FINDING OUR *love*

APHRODITE'S CASTLE | HOST CLUB

AMY TASUKADA

CONTENTS

ISBN ebook mobi: 978-1-948361-19-4
ISBN ebook epub: 978-1-948361-18-7
ISBN Paper: 978-1-948361-20-0

Cover Design: Natasha Snow
Content & Copy Editing: Lyss Em
Proof Read: Christy Editing
Interior Format: Rene Folsom

ACKNOWLEDGMENTS

Thank you to my family. Without your support, I wouldn't be able to have the time to follow my dream and write. Thank you to the Dallas Area Romance Author group. A lot of the plotting of this book took place during a writing retreat, so their input was greatly appreciated. Legne Hardt, your plotting help is magical and breaks through all of my blocks. Nell Iris and Addison Albright, thank you for always being my go-to writing buddies. A special thanks goes out to Michelle and Ash for your early reading comments. Also to all my readers: thank you for taking a chance to read my book.

The card had looked so harmless taped in Iroha's birthday card. Its golden swirls against matte black spoke of a luxury Iroha's budget didn't often allow, but then he'd read the note.

Maybe you'll have better luck finding Mr. Right here.

His cheeks still burned thinking about it.

Iroha tapped the plastic card against his fingers and stepped into the elevator. A new set of paints would've been more useful than a membership to a host club. Still, obligation forced Iroha to visit the club once. Then he could cut up the card and use the bits in some mixed-media piece.

He smashed the button labeled Aphrodite's Castle Host Club and pushed up his dark-framed glasses.

The golden doors closed, and he flicked off a few paint flakes from his long black hair. He'd refused to buy a suit for a gift he didn't ask for, so he wore the only pair of pants without any paint on them. Sure, the red plaid and spiked belts looked more appropriate for an evening at a rock concert, but maybe he'd give the old businessmen at the club heart attacks.

Iroha smirked. Then they'd ask him to leave, and he could avoid the awkward conversation with Mr. Sakai about why he never went back.

The doors opened, and Iroha's eyes narrowed. The elevator hadn't budged.

He pressed the button. Again.

It lit up.

The doors shut.

The elevator didn't move.

He glanced around. Maybe the host club had a hidden camera to filter clients before they could enter. He wouldn't be so lucky. Considering how powerful Mr. Sakai was, Iroha could cosplay Astro Boy and they'd still treat him like a VIP.

The doors opened. Iroha groaned and slapped the button.

Operating an elevator couldn't be so complicated. He felt more like an idiot than when his junior high math teacher had called out his score. If there was a hidden camera, the people watching were laughing.

He slammed his fist against the side of the panel. Pain shot through his hand, but it felt good. Even if the elevator won, at least Iroha felt like it knew his wrath. He rubbed his palm and caught sight of a light on the side of a black hockey puck hidden underneath the buttons. Iroha brought the plastic card on top of the puck and the light switched from red to green. He pressed the floor button, and the elevator climbed.

His nerves twisted like an octopus tentacle tickling his stomach.

He needed a smoke.

He reached into his pocket and pulled out a lollipop. He shouldn't have quit smoking until after fulfilling the obligatory gift. Suckers were supposed to help with the mouthfeel he'd miss. At least it was cherry flavored. He unwrapped the sweet and clanked it between his teeth.

Nowhere near the same mouthfeel, but at least it satisfied his sweet tooth.

The doors opened, and the scent of roses plucked him from the elevator. Yet, instead of stepping into a sea of old gay men singing off-key karaoke, he stood in a glossy-floored entry. His thick-soled boots clanked against the wood. An explosion of red and white roses stood in the center of a rounded sofa. The tufted emerald velvet contrasted with the clean lines of the host stand.

The décor only kept his attention so long. It was pretty but nothing original. Then the sapphire shadows of the room shifted to amethyst. They drew his gaze above the sofa to the blown glass chandelier.

"It can't be the real deal." Iroha kneeled on the sofa and craned his neck to inspect the swirled glass.

His mouth dropped open, and the candy sucker smacked against his teeth. The effortless curves and playful design looked authentic, but it couldn't be a real Chihuly. A simple vase would've been an expensive luxury, but a full chandelier probably cost as much as the yearly rent for the club.

It had to be fake. A damn good fake, but still a fake.

He needed to know the creator. Plenty of clients were looking for cheaper alternatives.

"Do you have an appointment?"

Iroha turned to the voice, noticing for the first time a man behind the host desk in a standard white button-down shirt and black vest.

Iroha climbed off the sofa. "This is my first time here."

"Can I get your name?"

"Iroha Osumi."

A line creased the center of the man's brow. "You never filled out a profile."

"Someone bought the membership for me." Iroha rubbed the back of his neck.

"Excuse me while I get the manager."

The man left, giving Iroha enough time to change his mind about the Chihuly. No one could fake the curves. It had to be the real deal.

"I'm sorry for the delay, Mr. Osumi." The manager's deep voice turned Iroha's attention away from the chandelier. "I'm Subaru Kobayashi."

The thin cut of his vest pinched in at his waist and made him look more like someone from the American twenties down to his hat. His wide smile couldn't hide the fact he could break Iroha in two.

"Mr. Sakai is a good friend, so I will be personally handling your first visit to Aphrodite's Castle."

"Is that a real Chihuly?" Iroha pointed to the chandelier.

"You have a good eye, but I wouldn't suspect any less from such a talented artist."

Iroha cracked the lollipop in two. He was used to the

schmoozing at art shows, but at a host club he'd thought he could avoid it, since everyone involved knew the flirting and compliments the hosts whispered into their clients' ears were fake.

"Seems a bit excessive," Iroha said.

Subaru's smile sent a lump into Iroha's throat. Like he'd swallowed a liter of paint. Even the saccharine candy couldn't flush out the bitter taste.

"You'll find we spare no expense for our guests. Usually there's an extensive interview process before a guest is even allowed to see that Chihuly. A written application, then an interview, during which we construct a profile."

Didn't they want guests to come? Not that Iroha had attended any host clubs before, but Aphrodite's Castle seemed way too excessive for its own good.

"I assure you the precautions are for our guests' privacy. Many are well known and would appreciate their sexual preference not splashed across the front pages. If you tell me a bit more about the evening you'd like to experience, I'd be happy to make a suggestion."

Iroha shrugged. "Whatever."

"Perhaps you'd like to see who we have on offer?" Subaru handed Iroha a black tablet.

Iroha took the tablet and flipped through the profiles. It was one thing to judge someone based on their art portfolio but another thing altogether by their looks. Iroha rubbed his hand on his pants.

All the men on offer could've been out of a magazine, but after the third good-looking guy, they blurred together.

"What does it mean when it says 'Gold Room only' next to their picture?"

"To better accommodate our guests, we have two levels. The Gold Room is more of a bar or club atmosphere. The Onyx Lounge is quiet, and the host can keep only you as company. Of course, this privilege comes with a bump in membership, but Mr. Sakai provided those monthly fees for you."

Iroha nodded along and flipped through more of the photos attached to little bios he didn't read. There was no need to fake worrying about personality at a place like this. He stopped at one, captivated more by his suit than his face. Though that wasn't bad either. His burnt-orange dress shirt with a peacock-green tie made for a striking contrast to everyone he'd passed. The catalog called him Kenta. His black hair sensibly dyed with red highlights stood out against the various blonds.

"I'd like Kenta." Iroha handed back the tablet.

"Excellent choice. I'll get you set up in the Onyx Lounge—"

"Let's start with the Gold."

Mr. Sakai might've paid the membership fee but nothing else. The private room probably came with a price tag to match, and while Iroha made a comfortable income from his gallery, the bill for tonight would be his splurge of the month. If the manager was disappointed, he didn't show it.

"We need a card on file for the drink and host fee, and then your hour with Kenta can begin."

Iroha nodded and handed over the card. He might've not gone to a host club before, but he knew full well one wasn't supposed to use cards as payment. He should've suspected something shady from Mr. Sakai, but it wasn't like Iroha could claim to be completely innocent.

He handed over the card and, with a quick swipe, the manager gave it back.

"There are a few rules to keep in mind once you get inside. Never touch any of the hosts or ask personal questions. If a host ever feels uncomfortable, you will be escorted out and your membership revoked. At other host clubs you might've been to, you could pay enough and meet the host outside for sex. Not here. The hosts aren't even allowed to date clients. You understand?"

"Crystal."

"Good." The smiled returned to Subaru's face. "If you could make your way inside, Kenta will meet you at the bar."

The manager opened the gold door, holding it open for Iroha to walk inside. While the room wasn't huge, it had the same aesthetic as the front. Elegant but ordinary. Dance music played, and a color-changing floor had guest taking up most of the space. The cool color tones invited him in.

Iroha slid up to the bar, and the bartender strolled over. Even he looked out of a magazine page, with auburn hair styled in a heart, emphasizing his angled jaw. Iroha hadn't seen so many attractive men in one place.

"Would you like to see our menu, or do you have something in mind?" he asked.

Iroha shrugged. "Give me what's popular."

"A Love Potion it is."

The bartender tossed the glass, twirling it around

and flipping bottles. He handed Iroha a pink concoction. Iroha popped out the stick left from his sucker and put it in a nearby crystal ashtray. The urge to see if he could bum a cigarette off a host nagged at him, but he clutched onto the pink drink the bartender placed before him.

He took a sip. It tasted expensive, and Iroha thought of how he'd have to add a few extra zeros to the paintings hanging on his gallery walls if he made a habit of coming to the Castle.

Iroha snorted, the alcoholic sting crawling up his nose. There was no way he'd make a habit out of coming here.

"Hey, I'm Kenta." The man slid onto the barstool next to Iroha.

Kenta's cool voice had Iroha leaning in closer to hear. His collared vermillion shirt peeked out from beneath an aqua jacket. The lights might've been distorting the shade, but the combination drew in Iroha. He wasn't sure if it worked or not.

Kenta smiled, and his rounded face formed the most adorable dimples Iroha had seen. They made Kenta look more like the kid he'd had a crush on down the street than the slick-dressed cover model he appeared when relaxed.

"What's your name?" Kenta asked.

"The manager didn't tell you?"

"He only said I'd know you when I saw you."

"Iroha."

"That's different."

"Knowing my parents, they probably thought calling

me the equivalent of A-B-C would make a fun social experiment."

Kenta laughed, his laughing dimples a million times cuter than his smiling ones. "If you have hard feelings about it, I'm fine using your last."

Iroha waved his hand. It would be unfair since they were using Kenta's first name.

"Iroha is fine." He brought the glass up for another sip.

The music switched to a different song, the same steady thump vibrating through his body. Once the singer's electronic voice came on, phasing through the song, the silence between them grew to a chasm.

"What do you do?" Kenta asked.

"I own a gallery."

"That's different. Do you do any art then?"

"Painting mostly, but I've been playing around with 3-D printing."

Iroha forgot the times he'd had the exact conversation.

"My Dad would stencil a display on our store windows. Every time he'd do it, he'd say how he'd always wanted to be an artist and wished he could do it freehand."

The glint in Kenta's rosy brown eyes might've held some fond memory, but everyone was an artist. Sure, they were at different places along the path, but no kid didn't have their parents shoving crayons into their hands. Not picking up the box again was their own fault.

"How do you choose your colors?" Iroha gestured to Kenta's clothes. "The combination is unique."

Kenta laughed.

"What's so funny?"

"I never thought an artist would say I put colors together well."

"They might be different, but I like different."

"So do I." Kenta's smile made Iroha's heart thump in time with the music. The words Kenta had probably said to many people before. He was a host after all. Iroha cleaned his hand on his pants. This was what the host was paid for: making him seem like the most interesting person in the world. Iroha had been to enough opening shows to recognize the false flattery, but Kenta did it so well.

Kenta tugged at his sleeve. "I'm color blind, so half the time it looks gray or brown."

"Really?"

"Would you like something else to drink?" Kenta asked.

"Yeah, that would be nice."

Kenta flagged down the bartender. "Is there anything specific you'd like? Hiroya has a flare for making some nice mixed drinks, but we offer a lot of tasty wines too."

"The love potion was good."

"If you like that, then can I make a suggestion?"

"Sure."

"May I drink with you?"

"Yeah."

Kenta ordered something called Athena's Dream.

"So everything you see is gray?"

"Blues and yellows are fine. It's the reds and greens that are off."

"What about purple?"

"It's hard to say. It looks like blue, maybe different." Kenta shrugged. "I can't tell how it's supposed to look."

"So you see the world different than other people."

"A lot of people are color blind. Maybe some don't like to say it, but it's me."

Iroha bit his lip, then he realized. It was probably what everyone else asked him. Like the long list of questions about his family when he met anyone familiar with the art community.

The green drink was delivered with an orange slice on the side and a rim of salt.

"This one is fun. It has all the flavors. You drink, lick the salt, then suck on the orange."

"This is different."

"You'll love it." Kenta grinned. "If not, then you can punish me."

Kenta grabbed his glass and yelled "cheers" before the words caught up with Iroha.

They downed the drink. A little sweet with a bite. The salt the perfect twist, and the taste of the orange a refreshing finish. They put their drinks down. Iroha's was almost empty and Kenta's about half.

"Ah, you beat me."

A light buzz flooded Iroha's head.

"You like to dance?" Kenta asked.

Iroha shook his head. "Not really. This isn't my kind of music."

Kenta held up his glass. "What is your kind of music then?"

"Visual kei band called Lillith." Iroha tugged at his

necklace. "No one really knows the band. I like their aesthetic."

"Their She-Creature Tour looks were the best. Jin and those huge horns."

"Did you see them on tour when they were here in summer?"

"I had to work."

"They put on an awesome show. The recordings don't do it justice."

"Really? I'll have to get a ticket when they come again. Are you in the fan club?"

Iroha's eyes grew wide. "Of course. That's how I was able to snag the tickets. I think my friend and I were the only men there."

"What did you think of when they switched from the paper to the digital version of the magazine?"

The conversation flowed so easily Iroha no longer needed to lubricate it with alcohol.

The manager came over and whispered something to Kenta

"I need to get going, but this was an awesome time. I'll see you around soon?"

"Already?"

"It's been an enjoyable three hours, but my next client is expecting me." Kenta stood.

"That long?"

Kenta glanced down, then back up to meet Iroha's eyes. The single look collapsed Iroha's lungs and sent splattering white spots around Kenta. Everything burned up in his brilliance.

"I'll see you later, Iroha."

His chest unlocked and breath flooded back only for him to catch Kenta walking away. His hand in his pants pocket lifted the back of his blazer to show off a perfect butt.

Iroha tilted his head, licked his lips, and crossed his legs to hide his excitement.

Shit.

He wanted to see Kenta tomorrow and the day after. He doubted the gallery could keep up with the price of his desires.

2

Kenta slid his finger over each of the mah-jongg tiles in front of him. Winning was impossible so late in the game, but he could lessen the burn of defeat by making the right choice so he wouldn't be the only one paying.

He glanced back over the discard piles of his opponents. They'd varied the suits. Something Kenta still hadn't mastered, which probably added to his lack of wins. Though his three lady opponents in front of him had at least sixty years of experience on him, so it was impossible to catch up.

He tapped the seven bamboo, checking if the others of the set were given up or kept.

"Have you found a boyfriend yet?" Granny Omi asked.

"Granny!" Kenta's cheeks grew hot like he'd spent the day hiking.

"Well, it has been awhile since you've dated that one guy. What was his name?"

Mei poked Kenta's bicep with the dull end of her knitting needle. "And you go to the club all the time. You must find lots of attractive men there."

"We're not allowed to date our clients."

"It's always easier to beg forgiveness than to ask permission." Tomoko's grin made it clear she spoke from experience. "It's like the day when one of my friends broke into the morphine—"

Mei and Granny Omi groaned in unison, reminding Tomoko they'd heard the story earlier in their game. She laughed off her failing memory and smiled in a way that made Kenta hope he'd be as joyous at eighty-three.

The playful joking was why Kenta always came to the nursing home before heading to work. Sure, his clients were interesting, but none of them had stories like the ladies. Even when Granny Omi was his parents go-to babysitter back in their small village, she'd always had new stories to tell.

"I've seen Subaru when he's thrown out clients. Best not to make the boss angry." Kenta discarded one of his mah-jongg tiles.

"*Ron*," Granny Omi called, snatching Kenta's tile and showing off her winning hand.

"I'm going to have to take out a loan with this losing streak," Kenta joked.

"You shouldn't have to worry about money. You always wear those nice suits all the time. Why aren't you like that today?" Tomoko asked.

"It's Monday, so I get to go home for a few days after I pick up my paycheck, remember?"

"You don't have any good news for your parents?"

Granny Omi asked. "Ever since you got embarrassed when your mom asked if you were practicing safe sex with your high school crush, she thinks you hide your boyfriends from her."

Seven years ago, and she still brought it up like it happened yesterday. He should've been happy they were only pushing him to finally get a long-term relationship while other parents their age would be pushing for grandkids.

"I don't have time to date." Kenta rubbed his hands against his jeans, and Omi shot him one of her *I-know-you're-hiding-something* looks. "There was an interesting client the other day."

"Was he cute?" Mei asked.

"He had this long crow-black hair that stuck out like a lappet moth caterpillar."

Kenta's toes curled, remembering how the thin chain of Iroha's necklace had dangled across his collarbone, begging to be licked. Iroha had played with it while they'd chatted, and each time he'd dropped the chain, Kenta's gaze had glued to Iroha's exposed neck.

So many of Kenta's clients wore collared shirts underneath heavy suits, but not Iroha.

"With that look in your eye, I think you can figure out a way to hide dating from your boss." Tomoko elbowed Kenta.

He sighed. "It doesn't matter. He didn't seem like the type who would come back."

"Then you wouldn't have to worry about hiding your dates."

At least they'd stopped trying to get him to go out

with whatever nursing home resident had a grandson who'd come out of the closet.

Kenta's phone alarm buzzed, reminding him he needed get to the station.

"My time is up here, ladies. How much do you I owe you this time?"

Kenta paid and pulled his weekend bag over his shoulder.

Granny Omi handed a stack of envelopes to Kenta. "Could you deliver these for me, sweetie?"

"Of course."

Kenta hugged them goodbye and slipped Omi's letters inside his bag. He waved to the nurses at the front and walked out. It was a quick bus ride to the host club.

Monday was payday and the start of Kenta's weekend off. He'd pick up his money and take the train back to his home village. He'd arrive in time for dinner and would spend the rest of his time off helping his parents with their grocery store.

Kenta sneaked behind the building and climbed the stairs to avoid any waiting clients. Even if none of them were his, they might've spotted him at the club before, and Kenta's relaxed jeans and tank weren't within dress code. On his weekends he didn't even bother sending Teru an outfit shot to make sure he wasn't wearing a strange color combination.

He knocked on the back door until Daigo opened. He stood shorter than Kenta, and the baseball cap and pajamas he was wearing weren't the standard uniform either.

"Subaru says the top hosts are different." He pulled

up his hat and slicked back his spiky hair before putting the cap back on.

"You think someone finally toppled Ryuutaro's number one spot?"

Daigo snorted. "Impossible. I can't remember a time he hasn't been number one."

At the smaller host club Kenta had worked at, the top spots fluctuated weekly. The Castle, not so much, but the larger base salary made up for it even if most of it went into maintaining the lifestyle his clients expected. Most of Kenta's income came from receiving a percentage of what his clients bought. The large bonus of being in the top three went directly to his parents.

He'd found a steady spot of third place for the past six months, but if he'd finally moved to second, it would be a substantial increase. His parents needed a new heater. The one they'd used last year smelled like plastic. The extra bonus would get them a better model easily.

Daigo whistled from the doorway of the break room. "Stop daydreaming or you'll miss the announcement."

Kenta scurried over, clutching his bag and debating if he should tell his parents about their new heater or have it be a surprise.

The break room wasn't as luxurious as the front house, but the plush gray sofas were comfortable enough for a quick nap between clients. Hosts crowded the space, most dressed for work since getting the slow days off at the start of the week came from a mix of seniority and rank.

Subaru walked to the center, hat perched on his head

and a stack of thick envelopes in his hand. The first three were bright red for the top three hosts.

"Has the rumor gotten around about the shake-up in the top three?" Subaru asked with a laugh that broke his American gangster–looking façade.

It got a small chuckle from everyone.

"We always want to reward our hosts who put the extra effort into making sure their clients enjoy their time." Subaru started the speech he always gave. "To show our gratitude our top three hosts are given a substantial bonus. Our first place host this week is Ryuutaro."

Everyone clapped while Ryuutaro grabbed his envelope and lingered by the door. Usually he'd grab the cash and leave, but today he lingered, probably wanting to see what the big shake-up was.

"Now for the shake-up. The difference between our second and third rank hosts was only five thousand yen."

Kenta blinked. A simple suggestion of another drink was all the difference? Damn. One of his clients had let him pick whatever champagne he'd wanted. Kenta had chosen a more expensive option, so that had to be how he'd made it to number two.

His fingers tingled. If he was able to maintain the second rank, his parents could hire someone part-time. They'd had Kenta late in life. So while he was still in his early twenties, they were close to retirement. A part-time worker would help ease their workaholic tendencies.

"Our third ranking host was Daigo."

Everyone clapped. It was a shake-up if Daigo got third on top of Kenta reaching second.

Daigo took his envelope, wearing the biggest grin that Kenta had seen on his face in a long time.

Subaru held out one last red envelope. "That makes our second ranking host this week Hiroya."

The cheering faded into Kenta's ears. But Hiroya was always second. The shake-up was that Daigo had moved up to third.

Kenta swallowed, but the lump in his throat stayed like a bad cold. He'd gotten no bonus to give his parents.

"Thank you, everyone, for your service. Here's to an even better week." Subaru fanned out the other envelopes of cash on the table.

Kenta walked over to Subaru, who smiled at him sincerely, but it crushed Kenta even more.

"It's just one week," Subaru said. "One of Daigo's clients celebrated his birthday here, but there's always next week to get your third spot back."

Kenta picked at the edge of his bag's strap, reminding himself he went to Kyoto in the first place to help out his parents. He needed to be the kind of son they could depend on. He'd cancel his monthly shopping trip and give the money to his parents. He could cover one week's screwup.

"Can I look at my numbers?" Kenta asked.

"As always. Let's talk about it in my office."

He followed Subaru to his small office by the kitchen. Subaru typed away at the computer before sharing the screen listing Kenta's clients and their spending.

He scanned the clients, everything within his average until he got to Iroha. He'd spent less than anyone. Kenta's lips flattened, but then he sighed. He couldn't blame

Iroha. Kenta was the one who was supposed to sell him a fantasy fueled by expensive alcohol; instead he'd been too busy talking about music and staring at his collarbones.

"New clients can be hard to judge. Iroha is a VIP, and he walked out of here smiling, so you did your job," Subaru said.

Kenta's eyes grew wide. "You didn't tell me he was a VIP."

"You know how to do your job. Why would I need to tell you?"

VIPs weren't one and done clients. Iroha would come back, and Kenta wouldn't get too caught up in his own fantasy to sell him drinks. Maybe Iroha would be different.

"He hasn't made another reservation, has he?" Kenta asked.

"Not yet."

Good. He couldn't afford to see Iroha again.

3

Iroha had convinced himself working in the gallery's office would keep his mind off the mail delivery.

It didn't.

In fact, the windowed walls of the office framed the front door like a still life. He would've titled it *The Slow Demise of a Failing Artist*, and all the critics would have said his sister would have done it better.

The rock ballad faded from his computer speakers and switched to the death screech from the vocalist of Lillith. Then a hard thump from the bass set the stage for the high-adrenaline song *Blood Pride*. Kenta had said it was one of his favorites, then he'd shot Iroha a dimpled smile. Iroha had eaten up every last one of those, and after Kenta had left, Iroha had figured he'd had his fill. With the song playing, the little nudge to see Kenta again crept in like shared melody of the song's twin guitars. It would be an easy few clicks to set up another date.

Date?

Not a date.

Dates didn't come billed by the hour. But Iroha had had a better time talking with Kenta than he'd had during any other dates he'd been on.

When had he become so pathetic?

If one simple Lillith song got him already ranking Kenta as the best date of his life, then Iroha was in trouble.

He had to get unpathetic if he wanted to see Kenta again, and that meant returning to submitting to galleries under his real name. The past year, he'd had the bright idea to prove people enjoyed his art for his talent and not his familiar connections, but every gallery he'd submitted to had sent him rejections.

He should've been happy the galleries still sent him rejection notes instead of ignoring him completely. He still had one submission out though, and the gallery's response was due back any day now. If they said yes, he could celebrate with a visit to Aphrodite's Castle. A quick hour with only one drink wouldn't be too expensive. Kenta would understand his lack of spending.

The door chimed.

Iroha shot up from his chair, but instead of the mail carrier, a dozen five- to six-year-olds flooded inside. Their teacher, Chiyoko, came in behind them. Her amethyst-colored dress resembled the cool tones of Kenta's jacket. Iroha rubbed his forehead and tossed his pencil onto his desk. He couldn't lounge around and think about Kenta all day.

"Look!" One of the kiddos ran to the back-wall display.

Iroha smiled and followed the rest of the group to the

back wall. They pointed at their watercolorworks from the previous week hanging on the wall beside the works for sale.

Iroha's gallery hadn't always been successful. After the big opening, foot traffic had slowed, and he hadn't sold enough art to cover the mortgage. A prestigious preschool was a few blocks away. It was the kind where parents filled out resumes for their kids to be judged by, and the school promised everything from English classes to violin lessons. Iroha had used the Osumi name to get a meeting with the principal, and from then on, half his mortgage had been paid and the school had been able to add weekly classes to their list of offers.

The lessons explored different art mediums and focused more on fun than technique. For the most part, art was subjective, and in a few years, the children's purple giraffe-cat hybrids would be frowned upon. Iroha only hoped the art-equals-amusement foundation he'd built within them would propel them through the soul-crushing grind of art theory.

The kids were always excited to see their art hanging up and would often make their parents come see the weekly display change. Most of the time, the parents would see a piece that caught their eye and make a purchase before leaving.

"Happy late birthday," Chiyoko said, the children saying it after her.

Heat radiated throughout Iroha's chest, and he squatted down, making it easier for each child to hand him a sucker using the proper etiquette under Chiyoko's watchful eye. She must've taught them before they'd walked over.

Iroha thanked each one and filled his pockets with the suckers.

"When I told them it was your birthday the other day, they all wanted to get you something."

Iroha laughed. "Well, it was quite the surprise. I'll be stocked for days."

"And I got you this." She pulled out a wrapped, booked-shaped gift from her bag and offered it to Iroha.

"You didn't have to."

"You said you hadn't read it yet. You need to. It's so good."

His hands clenched around the edge of the book, taking in the familiar size. Hopefully, it was just one of the many books Chiyoko had recommended and not the one it felt like.

"I'm sure I'll love it." Iroha faked a smile. "I'll put it away, then we can get the kids started."

"Come on, children, let's see what Mr. Iroha has for us to create today." Chiyoko shuffled the kids to the back studio as Iroha dumped the book onto his desk.

"Finger paint!" Iroha said.

The kids jumped up and down, and Chiyoko shot Iroha a *you-don't-have-to-listen-to-their-parents-complain* glare.

"And no matter how much they scrub, they come away with paint under their fingernails."

"All artists have paint underneath their fingernails."

Another glare.

"Fine. I'll give them extra time to wash up. Besides,

the kids enjoy it more than anything else, and art is supposed to be fun."

They suited up the kids in trash bags with holes cut out for their limbs and set them at the table to paint. In a matter of minutes, they were in their painting element.

"I love the movement you have going here," Iroha said to one of the kids.

"I don't have a green," the kid said.

"Why don't you try mixing some colors together and see what you get?"

Iroha limited their color choices to magenta, cyan, and yellow. So the kids got some modern color theory thrown in without realizing it.

The door chimed.

The mail.

Iroha's heart sparked, sending a jolt down his spine. He poked his head out the door and narrowed his eyes. It wasn't the mail carrier at all but Masahiro. He strutted inside, lit up a cigarette, and examined the newest art on display.

Iroha told Chiyoko he was heading outside and caught up with Masahiro.

"Outside?" Iroha asked.

Masahiro shrugged, his pinstripe blazer making his broad shoulders even more square, but he followed Iroha outside. Masahiro offered Iroha a cigarette, but Iroha shook his head.

"Still trying to quit?" Masahiro's deep voice sounded rough as a bar fight.

Iroha unwrapped one of the suckers. "So far it's been working."

"Didn't think it would work."

"Last time I helped your boss get a painting, I was there for the cleaning and saw how much gunk was caked from cigarettes." Iroha shuddered. "It was disgusting."

"Mr. Sakai wanted me to check that you had a good time at Aphrodite's Castle."

"It was good."

"Good." A long stream of smoke blew out of Masahiro's nose. "Nice to see you playing the field."

"I don't think paying someone to hang out with me is playing the field."

Masahiro's deep laugh melted away his scary yakuza exterior. "It's a start for you. Your previous method of ordering art supplies online and locking yourself in your studio wasn't working."

Iroha chose not to answer and tongued the sucker to the other side of his mouth, the sweet not dampening his craving with Masahiro smoking away right there.

"Anyway, Kawata's out of rehab, and Sakai wants you to put on a showing next week so he can bring a few people to admire the art."

Mr. Sakai had rescued Iroha from closing his gallery and moving back with his parents. Kawata, Mr. Sakai's nephew, had finished art school, and Mr. Sakai wanted him to be successful. So anytime Mr. Sakai decided Kawata needed to put on a show, Iroha made it happen. Mr. Sakai would bring in customers who bought no matter what price Iroha stuck there. Iroha got his commission and handed the money to Masahiro, who gave it to Kawata. There was probably something fishy going on, but Iroha tried not to think about it too much.

"Next week?" Iroha said. "That's not enough time for anyone to paint a whole show."

"I'm not even an artist, and I know Kawata can bang out those paintings in an afternoon. If anything, I could paint them, and no one would know the difference."

Kawata's paintings were more glorified paint samples than art. If Mr. Sakai and Iroha hadn't struck up the agreement, Iroha would've rejected everything Kawata submitted.

Smoke swirled around Masahiro. "I think he wants to keep Kawata busy so he doesn't start using again."

Iroha nodded. "I'll go check on him tomorrow and get the arrangements made."

The wind picked up, and the rustle of papers drew Iroha's attention to a stack of mail beside the gallery wall.

"Is that my mail?"

Masahiro took a puff from his cigarette. "I think the guy got spooked when he saw me coming."

Iroha scooped up the pile and thumbed through it until he found the letter from the gallery.

"Is that the one you were telling me about?" Masahiro asked.

Iroha clutched the envelope, trying to the response determine by the thickness.

"Go ahead and open it."

He tore the envelope open and read, but it only took the first few lines to understand the rejection. He crumbled up the paper. It meant all of them. A whole year of submitting had left him with nothing but rejection.

"Fuck those guys," Masahiro said. "You make more in commission selling one of Kawata's paintings than that guy could in a month."

"That's not the point."

Masahiro put a hand on Iroha's shoulder. The kids started to file out, each saying goodbye with a thank-you.

"I gotta go," Iroha said.

Masahiro stubbed out the cigarette. "Call if you need me."

Iroha went back into his office and ripped open Chiyoko's gift. His sister's picture stared back at him next to one of her life-size, photo-realistic paintings of someone getting swallowed up by their bed. She'd created it when she was seventeen. Iroha had been a few months old when the painting had gone up for auction and shattered all the records.

He'd lived in Ichigo's shadow since the day he'd been born.

Iroha pressed his lips together and threw the book into the trash. The same place his career was without his family name attached.

If Kawata was painting again, Iroha could add an extra zero to his artwork, claiming he'd reached a bold new phase. Mr. Sakai's friends bought everything regardless of price.

Then at least Kenta could help him forget his failure.

Kenta's breath fogged in the twilight chill before dissipating. The gravel path of Oiso's Main Street opened before him. The hardware store and bookstore had closed long ago and reappeared as small sections in the aisles of his parents' grocery store.

If his parents were better businesspeople, they would've left Oiso ages ago, or at least his mom would have started charging for driving the villagers to doctors' offices. No wonder Kenta had flunked all his business classes.

He propped up his empty delivery bike next to the store. Making the rounds took all day since all the villagers wanted to gossip while Kenta unloaded their groceries. It was like he was at the host club all over again, except the villager didn't pay him by the hour.

The bell rang as Kenta entered the grocery store, but instead of the familiar greeting from his dad, there was silence. He wasn't even behind the counter.

"Dad!"

No response.

It wasn't like anyone would walk in and steal stuff. Most of the people in the village could barely walk to their mailbox, let alone the store, but his parents almost always made it a point to have someone behind the counter.

Kenta opened the store's back door leading to their family's living room.

Dad snored away on the sofa, the store's ledger rising up and down on his chest. Kenta let out a heavy breath. His father was too old to run the store all by himself, and with Mom driving the villagers to their doctors' appointments, the more the need for someone to be there pressed on Kenta.

He grabbed the ledger off Dad's chest and brought it back to the store. He'd helped his parents with the store's books on occasion, but lately they'd been having Kenta do something else whenever he brought it up.

Kenta sat in the chair behind the cash register and cracked open the ledger on the counter. His parents would never ask for more money. Heck, they didn't even ask for the money Kenta gave them. He'd stick it in the till, and they wouldn't talk about it. Looking at the books was the only way to tell what was really going on.

He conjured up the memory of accounting class, trying his hardest to not bring up all the red pen over his tests. He examined the columns. His throat grew drier the further he read.

Everything was being funded by the money he gave them. Why would they let it get so bad?

Not only had his parents not turned a profit in months, but they hadn't taken a salary all year.

The bell chimed as Mom entered.

"Done with the deliveries?" Mom asked. "What do you want for dinner?"

Kenta pointed to the ledger. "Why haven't you told me what was going on?"

"About what?" Mom glanced down at the figures. Her smile faded. "Don't worry. You give us everything we need."

"But what if something happened?"

"The nearest store is thirty minutes away, and no one else in the village can drive anymore. How else are they supposed to get food? We have to do what we can for the village."

Kenta shook his head. Mom was right, but still. "I'm going to go for a hike."

"It's too dark."

"I'll be fine."

Kenta left before his mother could get another word in, but night had descended fast on the village. Outside, the glazed-over lights of the store only lit the area around it.

Once he stepped outside the perimeter of the store, it grew dark. He couldn't wander the streets like he could in Kyoto when he needed to blow off steam. He sighed, turned on his phone's flashlight and walked.

The only thing Kenta could do was work his clients better. Ryuutaro always came first; maybe he'd give him some tips.

Kenta shook his head. Who was he kidding? Ryuutaro didn't talk to anyone who didn't pay. Unless he wanted to buy an hour of his time to probably only be talked into circles because Ryuutaro was more of a jackass and wouldn't help.

The buzz of the electric poles powered Kenta's thoughts. He'd broke down all the week's guests. They swirled around as he analyzed all the places he'd screwed up. Before he knew it, he came to the science research station outside the village.

The large gray metal building stood to the side of the valley. The building once housed the cafeteria for the workers. They'd ordered enough food from his parent's grocery store so his parents never had to worry about money. Kenta shined his phone's lights to bottom of the large sign marking the lab. A box with the keys was screwed underneath. Kenta pushed in the code and grabbed the keys.

"Might as well check out the cabins since I'm here," Kenta mumbled.

Along with the weekly delivery of Granny Omi notes, Kenta made sure the plants hadn't over taken any of the buildings.

A few dozen cabins dotted the space. Kenta unlocked the nearest one and clicked on the lights. The solar panels on the cafeteria roof still powered everything. Granny Omi's real-estate agent had convinced her that staging a few cabins would help sell the research facility faster. It didn't.

Kenta clicked on the lights. A fake plant sat on the little dining table and white linens covered the bed. The cabin looked like spring and stood in contrast to Kenta's warm breath fogging around him.

His phone buzzed and he checked the screen.

Are you okay? His mom texted.

Kenta sighed and typed. *I'm fine.*

It was almost midnight. Of course, she'd be worried. He'd been out for almost an hour.

He plopped onto one bed. The blow-up mattress pressed against his back in all the wrong ways. He had to do something to get his parents making a profit. It wasn't like he could convince anyone to buy some abandoned science lab.

If anything, he could prepare for his clients a little better. He flipped through his usual clients on Wednesday. Steady hours booked, all regulars. Then he scrolled to the last time slot at three in the morning.

Iroha.

He'd actually signed up again?

His collarbone flashed in Kenta's mind, making his cock stir.

Damn it.

Kenta had to get ahold of himself and pump Iroha for all the cash, not fantasize about his collarbones. Kenta licked his lips at the memory. They were nice collarbones.

His hand traveled down and he palmed himself through his pants.

Iroha was so different than his usual clients of high-powered salarymen who climbed the ladder so much they'd forgotten how to be kind. Sure, they treated Kenta well enough, but their egos had always rubbed against Kenta the wrong way.

But Iroha...

Iroha had no ego. The last thing he wanted to talk about was his art. He looked like one of the visual kei bands Kenta had hung on his wall as a teen. He moaned. It was like he'd dated a rock star. Kenta bit his lip. Not dating. Iroha was a client. There was no dating

Kenta had to treat him like all of his other clients. A super-hot, quirky artist client that he never had before. Kenta unzipped his pants and pulled out his cock. The cold air sent a chill down his spine. He wrapped his hand around his length, closing his eyes and pretended it was Iroha's.

He shouldn't be jerking off thinking about a client. Kenta's thumb swirled the pre-cum around his head, sending another shock of pleasurable heat through him. No. It was okay. He could fantasize about Iroha on his knees and swallowing him whole as long as he kept it a fantasy.

5

Kenta rubbed his eyes. He'd gotten used to staying up into the early hours of the morning, but the first day back was always the hardest. The ramp up in expensive hard-liquor drinking games might've helped host rankings but hadn't helped his pounding head.

He grabbed some medicine and gulped it down with a bottle of water. His empty stomach would hopefully help the meds kick in before Iroha arrived.

The overstuffed sofa called Kenta's name, and he sunk into it. One more hour, and his shift would be over. He'd be able to grab the first train and head home before sunrise if he was lucky.

He couldn't let the fog of a long night of drinking and lack of sleep cloud his focus. It would be easy to let the carefree feeling he got when talking to Iroha wash over him, but if he screwed up, he'd be stuck in fourth place and with no savings to pass along to his parents.

The next hour should be easy. He'd treat Iroha like the rest of the clients. He'd take him into the more expensive

Onyx Lounge. Then they'd start the drinking games. If things got off track, then he'd accidentally spill a drink.

Iroha knew what he was getting into when he crossed the elevator doors. Companionship came with a price and all the VIPs had money to burn.

Kenta rubbed the center of his chest. A tight knot lodged itself there like the mint leaves muddled at the bottom of an empty mojito. He wasn't going to call it guilt, even if that's what it was. Things clicked with Iroha differently than with any other client, differently than with any of Kenta's ex-boyfriends. If only they'd met outside the club, then things would be different.

"You're on fire today." Daigo plopped onto the sofa. "No way I'm cracking into the top three."

"I need the money."

"Isn't that always the case? One of my regulars said I always wear the same coats. Guess I'm picking up a new one next shopping trip."

Kenta rubbed his neck. "I'll probably have to cancel our usual trip."

"Come on. With the way you've been going, you'll earn your missed bonus back and then some."

"My parents have been lying to me about how the store's doing," Kenta said.

Daigo shrugged. "You said more and more people leave the village each month. It was only a matter of time, wasn't it?"

Kenta sighed. Daigo didn't get it. Probably because he'd grown up in the city. Everyone in the village might as well have been his family. His parents couldn't close shop.

How could they? They were the closet shop for a half hour. Most of the people in the village couldn't drive anymore, and some could barely walk around their houses let alone to the nearest bus stop. How would they eat without Kenta's weekly food delivery?

"I was hoping my parents could retire by then, but they are probably using their savings to buy everything they need." Kenta sighed.

"Sounds like you need a lot more cash."

"It'll be fine as long as I don't let any distractions slow my pace."

Daigo looked around. With no one around them, he leaned close. "Have you tried seeing clients outside the club?"

"And get fired?" Kenta's eyes narrowed.

"Subaru can't fire you if he doesn't know."

"Don't tell me you've dated clients?"

"We're not allowed to *date* clients. Sometimes we both happen to show up to the same place at the same time. It would be rude not to hang out."

"I can't believe it."

"It's just hanging out. We'll see a movie or get coffee, nothing crossing the line like a love hotel. Clients wouldn't come here if they were looking for prostitutes," Daigo said.

"And they pay you?" Kenta asked.

"That would be crossing the line."

"Then how is this helpful?"

"If they ask to hang out again, say you're busy and only have time to see them at the club. They'll get the hint, and when they return, ask for the most expensive wine. They understand where the cost comes from."

"Subaru would get pissed if he ever found out."

"It's hanging out. No dating. No feelings. You fall in love, then Subaru could tell. No matter how good you are, your other clients can tell, and then you're screwed as a host."

Subaru walked in, and Kenta's cheeks grew hot like he'd been breaking every rule and Subaru knew. He scanned the room and walked up to Kenta.

"Iroha's waiting for you at the Gold Room."

Kenta swallowed, but the tickling in the back of his throat stayed. He couldn't be stuck fourth on the list again, but seeing clients outside the club felt wrong. Aphrodite's Castle had treated him well. Why would he take a chance to blow it all away?

The music grew louder as Kenta approached the door to the bar. He opened the door, the newest dance mix playing; he'd already heard it a dozen times that night.

Iroha had a drink, so that was already a plus. He shrugged off a jacket, revealing a gray tank with a spattering of bright-blue paint along the side. A few speckled blue plaint dots danced up his left collar bone and up his neck. Kenta bit his lip. He'd never thought he'd want to lick paint before, but there he was imagining his tongue playing connect the dots.

"Glad you decided to come back so soon." Kenta kept his voice low, making Iroha lean in closer to hear.

Iroha pushed up his glasses. "It was fun to meet someone who likes Lillith as much as I do."

Kenta bit his tongue. They were not going to have a conversation about music again.

"What are you drinking?" Kenta asked.

"It's the Love Potion."

"Looks good." Kenta tapped the empty space where his drink would've been. He waited, almost seeing the wheels turn in Iroha's dark eyes.

His mouth dropped when he realized his mistake. "Let me order you something."

"Thanks."

Iroha grabbed the menu, looked at it, then rubbed his eyes before handing it to Kenta. "Why don't you order something you like? I stayed up late painting."

"I can tell." Kenta chuckled and gestured to Iroha's neck.

"I swear I took a shower. The paint gets everywhere."

"Hmm, I bet it does."

Kenta tried not to imagine naked Iroha covered in paint, but it was too late. There it was flashing in his mind and making him lick his lips. Iroha probably had sketchbooks full of nudes of his boyfriends. Kenta wouldn't have minded being another entry to the pages.

Kenta blinked. What was he thinking? He still hadn't ordered a drink, and there he was willing to pose nude for the guy. He had to stay focused.

"Three in the morning is an awkward time," Iroha said. "Do I just stay up late? Would it be better to get some sleep before waking up to spend time with you, then back to sleep? I did want to see you though, and this was the first available spot you had."

Kenta shook his head and pointed to his ear,

pretending he hadn't heard anything. "It's hard to hear you. Let's go to the other room."

Iroha tugged on the chain necklace he wore. "I really like this song here."

The techno beat was far from Iroha's music taste. Iroha looked down and poked more at the bottom of his empty drink (even his nails had paint underneath them). Had Kenta pushed him too far? Kenta had had shy clients before, but Iroha had been so cocky the first time. "I'm so bad. I still haven't gotten you that drink, sorry," Iroha apologized—again.

He flagged down Teru and ordered a refill, and the only thing Kenta could mumble was his usual. The prices he had memorized of every drink at Aphrodite's Castle had escaped when Iroha's shoulders had slumped inward. No. Iroha hadn't turned shy. Something was troubling him.

"Have you seen the new promotional video for Lilith?" Iroha asked.

"When did it come out?"

"Yesterday. Managed to snag the limited edition before it sold out."

Kenta groaned. "Already? Is the normal one still available?"

"It should be. I thought you were in the fan club. You didn't get the email?"

"No. I was back home, and my phone might as well be a doorstop there."

"In the country?"

"In this super tiny village called Oiso."

"Oiso?"

Kenta shook his head. "Unless you've lived there or are an arachnologist, there's no way you've heard of it. It's like two hours by train and a half hour by bus if you're lucky and it's running. They'll probably cut that line soon, no one goes anywhere close to there since the lab closed."

Kenta's mouth hung open with his last word.

He'd never told a client where he'd grown up. Sure, he'd say a small town, but he wouldn't name it. Kenta rubbed his head. How could he turn into such an idiot talking to some guy who couldn't get paint off his neck?

"An arachnologist?" Iroha asked.

"They study spiders. Oiso's big claim to fame is a unique subspecies of Joro spider. We even had a little lab of a few dozen scientist studying them in their natural habitat, but once the lab closed a few were taken to Shinshu University and that was that."

"Middle-of-nowhere villages can be nice, even ones crawling with spiders." Iroha laughed. "During the summers between semesters, I would take off to those middle-of-nowhere art colonies. I could forget who I was easily there."

Teru delivered their drinks. They both reached out for the same one at the same time. No. Kenta had reached out for Iroha's on purpose. Maybe it was stupid, but Kenta had to touch Iroha's hand. He had to know what it felt like, if the way they clicked could spark when they touched.

But it was too fast, and Iroha pulled away too soon, leaving Kenta's fingers craving more and his heart emptier than before.

"Sorry, go ahead," Iroha said.

They took their drinks, no hand-holding involved.

"Cheers." Kenta's voice sounded anything but cheerful.

They clinked their glasses together, and Iroha took a large gulp.

"There's something I've wanted to ask you," Iroha said.

"Go for it."

"Would you like to go to a gallery show?" Iroha asked.

Kenta hadn't expected that, but he didn't know what he was expecting. He wetted his lips, and out of the corner of his eye, he caught Subaru making his usual rounds. The way he looked at Kenta was like he knew everything.

"You're not asking me on a date, are you?" Kenta asked. "Subaru explained the rules, right? We're not allowed to date our clients."

"Of course not," Iroha said a bit too loudly. "I'm inviting everyone."

"Everyone?"

Iroha pulled out a stack of postcards from his jacket pocket and gave one to Teru. "You're invited too."

Teru cocked an eyebrow at Kenta, silently asking if Kenta wanted to see how far he could break the rules. Damn him and his stupid bartender ability to read people.

Iroha handed a postcard to Kenta. It had a few gray paintings in frames on the front with the show details on the back. He tapped his finger along the edge. Maybe Daigo was right. Maybe the reason Iroha hadn't wanted to go to the Onyx Lounge was that he wanted something a little extra. Then the next time he visited the club, he'd drop the cash Kenta needed him to.

"I don't know," Kenta said.

"I'll go," Teru said. "It looks fun."

"You'll love it. Kawata is a very popular artist."

Kenta bit the inside of his cheek. He couldn't rush into things. If Subaru found out, Kenta had no doubt he'd be fired.

"Everyone's invited?" Kenta asked.

"Yeah, I have posters and flyers in the usual spots."

Kenta grabbed the stack of postcards. "I can stick these in the back and try to get everyone to come."

Iroha rubbed his neck. "I mean, yeah."

"Okay, I'll do that."

Subaru couldn't fire everyone in the host club.

"So I'll see you there?" Iroha asked.

Kenta licked his lips. "Buy me another drink, and maybe I can be convinced."

The answer was yes. It wouldn't be anything but yes.

6

Iroha knocked on Kawata's apartment door. His art exhibition was in four days. Each day Iroha called, and each day Kawata's voicemail answered. Without Iroha's prodding, the show would've been a painting or two. Kawata might've been able to survive selling so few, but Iroha's commission wouldn't last more than a few weeks. If he wanted to keep his weekly visits to Kenta, there needed to be at least ten.

"Kawata, you there?" Iroha groaned and banged on the door.

If Kawata was too high to answer the door again…

Iroha dropped the bag of paint he'd picked up from the hardware store and grabbed the spare key from underneath the doormat. Kawata had been out of rehab how long? A week? And he had already been out partying hard enough he couldn't answer his door. It was two in the afternoon.

Iroha opened the door and returned the key to its hiding place. The aesthetic of Kawata's apartment matched his art—modern and with the personality of a cheap chain hotel. The only interesting features were the colorful bottles of expensive liquor littering the surfaces.

"Damn it." Iroha sighed.

He'd be lucky if Kawata had even one painting finished.

Kawata wasn't in the living or the bedroom, so Iroha wandered into the back studio.

A blank canvas rested on an easel. Empty bottles crowded a table along with a cracked paint palette. Kawata snored away on the sofa, his legs propped up on the cushions while his torso had slid to the floor.

At least he was in the studio. Iroha rubbed his temple. Where to even start?

Out of the corner of his eye, he caught sight of a pack of cigarettes. His nerves fired. Sure, he planned on quitting, but that was before he'd had to deal with Kawata's lack of work ethic. A lollipop wasn't going to do shit. He grabbed the pack, tapped one out, and lit it.

The first deep inhale struck him better than he'd ever remembered. His shoulders slumped, and the harsh edges of life smoothed over. He could handle Kawata. He'd been doing it for years. A blank canvas four days before a show was nothing.

"Hey, wake up." Iroha dropped the bag of paints and shook Kawata's leg. "You getting high already? You just got out of rehab."

Kawata groaned and rubbed his head. "I'm hungover, not high."

"I'm surprised you're not dead with so many empty bottles."

"I had some friends over the past few nights."

Iroha took a deep inhale from his cigarette and pushed up his glasses. Kawata fought to push himself back up the sofa, but he ended up sliding down. He sat on the floor like he'd meant to the whole time.

"Some friends." Iroha shrugged. "They didn't even help you clean."

"They're my friends, not my maid." Kawata's overplucked eyebrows knitted together like two angry tufts of rice.

"You'll be lucky if your maid stays after seeing this."

Iroha tapped off the ash from his cigarette into an empty glass.

"It's so good." Kawata crawled up and sat on the sofa.

At first Iroha didn't know what Kawata was talked about, but then he saw it. The only surface on the table not covered with bottles was his sister's book. Like she was some god who couldn't be defaced.

That's why Iroha wanted to see Kenta. There was something about Kenta's smile that made him forget who he was. The art community had had their eye on him since birth. They knew everything about him and had already decided what rumors to believe. No one wanted to know about him; it was always to get to his sister. Kenta was the first person who never asked about her.

Iroha had had enough trouble ignoring the reporters who'd wanted a quote the past month.

What did he think of the book? Would he comment on the rumors surrounding them and their relationship?

Fuck them.

Iroha grabbed a few bottles and placed them on the

book. If he never saw the book again, it would still be too soon.

"Her book was the first thing I bought when I got out," Kawata said.

"How nice." Iroha rolled his eyes. "How's the paint—"

"Maybe that's why I can't get inspired? I look at her art, and it hits me." Kawata rubbed his hand over his heart. "Like she sees inside my soul and knows what's been haunting me, and she makes me face it."

"Yeah, well, that's her. You can't compare her art to yours. You can only compare your art to you."

"And you lived with her." Kawata shook his head. "How can you even lift a paintbrush?"

"You're starting a white phase?" Iroha gestured to the empty canvas, trying to steer the conversation back to Kawata's lack of work.

"I haven't felt inspired."

People didn't need to be inspired for the kind of art Kawata produced. They were usually paid minimum wage and completed a house in the time it took Kawata to feel inspired to paint a canvas blood red.

"Sometimes you gotta start, and then inspiration finds you," Iroha offered.

Kawata shook his head. "That might work for you, but it doesn't for me."

"Then go out. Go to the museum, see a movie, go find your inspiration."

Iroha couldn't believe he was talking about finding inspiration to a man whose biggest innovation in his art was adding a differently colored square into his solid pieces.

"I don't want anyone else to influence me. You know, don't you get that way when you see art at a museum?"

Iroha wanted to scream but knew better than to yell at his meal ticket. There were so many other artists with shows lined up at his gallery he'd rather visit. They wouldn't feed him some line about inspiration. They had real talent.

"Your big comeback show is in four days. It's a new chapter in your art. Everyone is excited to see what you're going to create."

"Really?" Kawata's eyes lit up.

Iroha had never met an artist less critical of their work than Kawata. Stroking his ego proved to be the best motivation.

"Of course," Iroha said. "It's been months since they've last seen you. They want to see how you've grown."

That perked up Kawata enough to get off the sofa and dump some red paint onto a palette. He stared at the white canvas.

Iroha took another long drag of the cigarette.

Kawata dabbed the brush into some of the paint and motioned toward the canvas, then pulled away.

"I don't know," Kawata said. "You know, when the mood isn't there, it just isn't there."

Iroha tapped his foot. "Maybe you need to try something new. You had your red phase for a while. So maybe it's time to experiment."

"But red's my favorite color, and it has such passion behind it and all the different shades."

"I know, but maybe looking at these can give you a new look at how they act next to red."

The cigarette dangled on Iroha's lower lip as he squatted and opened the paint cans. Since Kenta couldn't see red, Iroha had wanted him to be able to see some of Kawata's art.

Iroha popped the lid off a nice sky blue, then a vibrant yellow. It reminded him of the stripes on a Joro spider.

After he'd seen Kenta and gotten some sleep, Iroha had spent a few minutes researching Kenta's hometown. It had been a blip on the online maps. When he'd zoomed in on the town, it had been too pixelated for him to see anything but the greens of the trees. The only information that had come up in searches had been a few lines about the science lab and Joro spiders. Iroha sighed. It made him feel a little closer to Kenta even if their relationship wasn't going anywhere.

Iroha had sketched out a few spiders before he'd decided to go check on Kawata. Iroha could've been at home painting.

"Wow! Look at the yellow," Kawata said.

Iroha reached for the brush. "May I?"

He painted a little red square, mimicking Kawata's usual, then grabbed another brush and painted a yellow square beside it.

"Here, stand back and see," Iroha said. "Doesn't the yellow bring new life to the red?"

It was bullshit, but it might work enough for Kawata.

Iroha stepped back and watched Kawata's face. His rice eyebrows rose, but then his mouth opened. He turned to Iroha, nodded, and gave him a hug Iroha wanted no part of.

"You're amazing." Kawata's sincere tone almost made Iroha smile until Kawata said, "It's that Osumi blood in you."

Iroha hid his grimace. "You'll be good, then?"

"Yeah!"

"I know we usually aim for seven paintings at a show, but let's try ten. A lot of people are waiting for your return. You think you can do it?"

"If you think I can, I'll give it my best."

Iroha would talk to Masahiro about checking in on Kawata and kicking his butt if more of his friends wanted to come over for another party.

"I'll let you get to it, then," Iroha said, then left. He had his own painting to do.

7

Kenta and Teru walked down a boutique- and café-lined street to Iroha's gallery. No one else at the club had thought spending a few hours before work at an art gallery was worth their time. At least Teru had accepted the invitation so Subaru couldn't accuse Kenta of going on a date with a client. They'd go, look at some paintings, talk with Iroha a little bit, and leave with plenty of time left for Kenta's usual prework mah-jongg game with the senior ladies.

"You've climbed Mount Fuji, haven't you?" Teru asked.

Kenta could almost smell the crisp air at the summit just thinking about it. "A few times."

"My dad keeps thinking it would make a fun family vacation."

"It's a steady climb, and the view is pretty from the top."

"But you go hiking all the time. I don't think my feet could take it."

Kenta patted Teru's shoulder. "Wear the right shoes, and you'll be fine. There's even a bus that will take you halfway up if you think you'll need it."

Teru laughed. "Dad would call that cheating."

"It was our senior class trip, and everyone lived."

"You guys didn't do anything fun?"

"We were lucky to scrounge together ten students from the surrounding villages in my class. It was the only thing the school could afford."

"Must've been rough. There was no way you could hide in the back row and hope the teacher didn't call on you."

"Even worse, there were so few teachers that you'd be stuck with the same one for seven years. They'd remember that time when you were ten and failed all your kanji tests and would keep bringing it up."

Teru shook his head. "I couldn't live in the country."

Kenta laughed. "It wasn't too bad, but I wouldn't want to move back there."

"No galleries in the country?"

"None at all."

"What's this visit really about?" Teru asked with an *I-already-know-the-answer* tone in his voice.

Kenta tugged at his blazer sleeve. "I thought it would be fun."

"You've never seen anyone outside the club."

"Because most of them do office jobs that don't host public events."

"So instead of thinking up ways to get more money out of your highest-paying clients, you're spending time with your lowest?"

Kenta narrowed his eye. "Who told you Iroha was my lowest?"

"I'm the bartender. I know when you're too busy staring at a client and forget about charming them to order more drinks."

"Was it that obvious?"

"Subaru could've been standing right behind you, and you wouldn't have noticed."

Kenta rubbed his face to avoid Teru's judging gaze, but it didn't work. Kenta's own guilt hit him harder than any of Teru's glances.

"You think Iroha noticed?" Kenta asked.

"You both were like lovesick puppies."

Kenta's heart fluttered like a butterfly trapped in a spider's web. No. He wasn't the trapped insect. He was the spider luring Iroha into his web.

"I'm only going because it will convince Iroha to buy more drinks the next time he's at the club," Kenta said.

"That's a horrible idea, and you know it."

"Daigo says it works."

"And Daigo's on his last strike with Subaru for pulling shit like that."

"Oh."

"Why are you taking advice from Daigo anyway? You've earned more than him since the beginning." Teru smiled. "You're better off just admitting to yourself you're falling for Iroha."

"Have you been to a gallery show before?" Kenta stretched out his arms with a pretend yawn. "I wonder what it's like."

"You're avoiding the topic."

"I know the rules."

Kenta wasn't going to fall in love. Relationships never worked when he was a host. All his exes had gotten jealous, or the few times he'd dated a fellow host, they'd never had time to see each other.

Iroha's gallery stood at the end of the block. The letters *ABC* dripped into droplets of paint dotted the front door with the word *gallery* written underneath. Kenta had imagined the art gallery scene to be filled with people as vibrant as Iroha, but when he stepped inside, he might as well have entered a board meeting. Middle-aged salarymen lined the walls as much as the art.

Teru headed straight for the back table filled with booze and canapés, and Kenta followed.

"Not a bad spread." Kenta grabbed one of the open champagne bottles and poured them both a flute.

The white walls made the artwork stand out, but the paintings looked more like blocks on the wall. Kenta had imagined the art being more like what he saw in museums.

He stood in front of a painting that was a solid gray with a shocking yellow square at the bottom.

"I don't know about this," Kenta mumbled to Teru.

"What do you mean?"

Kenta jumped. It wasn't Teru at all, but some young guy with drawn-on eyebrows.

"You scared me. I thought you were my friend." Kenta glanced around, but Teru was nowhere to be found.

"What were you saying?"

Kenta rubbed his neck. "I'm not the art type."

"Anyone can appreciate good art."

"I'm color-blind, so I could be missing something, but it looks simple. This couldn't take more than like thirty minutes to paint."

"You wouldn't know good art if it bit you on the ass!"

"Kenta!" Iroha stepped between them. "I see you met the artist of this work, Kawata. His art is enjoyed by many people. He's one of my top sellers."

Kenta's jaw dropped. "I'm sorry. I didn't—"

Kawata turned up his nose. "You can't even see right. Why are you even here?"

Iroha's eyebrows narrowed. He gestured toward a group on the opposite side of the gallery. "Kawata, I think that guy bought one of your last paintings. Why not go talk with him?" Iroha seemed to not even try to soften the anger in his tone, but Kawata appeared oblivious.

Kenta downed the rest of his drink, and Kawata walked off. Maybe he was right. Maybe Kenta couldn't appreciate art.

"I'm sorry about him," Iroha said. "Kawata's a prick. Don't listen to anything he says."

Kenta stared back at the piece. "He's probably right. You have a whole showing for him. He must be good."

"He gets shows because he sells." Iroha dismissively waved his hand. "Here, maybe you'll like these more."

Iroha pushed up his glasses and walked toward the back of the showroom. Kenta followed. Usually Iroha's clothes had a *visual-kei-band-who-went-major-and-stopped-wearing-makeup* vibe, but for the show, he wore tailored slacks and a blazer that hit his ass at the perfect spot.

Iroha stopped in front of a small display labeled

"Future Artist of Kyoto" at the top with a dozen finger paintings underneath.

Kenta smiled. "These are so cute."

"I teach art for the day care down the block. They come by every week, and it's a lot of fun."

"This art I understand." Kenta pointed. "That's a butterfly, that's a kitty, and that's a giraffe. Or at least I think it's a giraffe."

Iroha laughed. "The artist indeed told me it was a giraffe, but with art it's about going with your gut and accepting your feelings. If you don't like it, it's okay."

Kenta glanced back to Kawata schmoozing up a crowd around him. "You said he was your best-selling artist."

"Modern art isn't for everyone. It's not my favorite either, but even if I don't like it, other people do. I'm not going to criticize their taste. I want to give them the space to appreciate whatever they like." Kenta nodded along to Iroha's words even if he sounded pained as he said them.

"So you're saying I should enjoy what I like and not worry what others think." Kenta smiled, hoping it would put Iroha at ease.

"Exactly. Maybe once this is over, we can..." Kenta's voice softened as a gentleman approached.

"I'm interested in buying one of the paintings," the man said. "Kawata said you were the person to talk with."

"Let me show you to the office." Iroha turned back to Kenta. "I'll find you again after I get this taken care of."

Kenta spent a few more minutes identifying most of the creatures the children had painted, then wandered off to find Teru staring at one of Kawata's paintings: a dark-gray canvas with a slightly darker gray square and a few dots of yellow.

"Maybe it's more symbolic," Teru said.

Kenta nodded. "Like the gray is the tainted society, and the yellow dots are the people who could break free."

"It's red, Kenta."

"Oh."

Teru shook his head. "Maybe we need another drink to understand."

A few drinks, tons of staring, and lots of listening to what others said about the paintings helped the time pass. One by one, Iroha placed dots on the info cards of the paintings to mark them as sold. The crowd thinned, and each time Iroha walked over, Kenta's heart would thump against his chest like an awkward finger-painted rabbit, but then someone would pull Iroha back into his office.

"I gotta get going and set up the bar," Teru said.

Kenta glanced at Iroha in his office, getting the paperwork set up for another sold painting. There was no way Subaru was ever going to consider their three-minute talk a date.

Kenta sighed. "I guess I should go too."

"You still have plenty of time. Setting up the bar takes a while, and today is inventory day. Subaru has me there extra early so we can go over the numbers."

Teru said a quick goodbye and left, leaving Kenta more alone. He'd seen all the paintings dozens of times, and none of them jumped out with their hidden meanings. Every time he'd get close to convincing himself, his biggest form of entertainment turned into finishing off the nearly empty bottles of champagne.

Iroha walked out of his office, following behind the last of the businessmen. He walked out the door, then locked it shut and sighed.

"Sorry," Iroha said. "I wanted to talk with you more, but all those interruptions. I was hoping we could paint together."

Kenta laughed. "I can't paint."

"Everyone can paint. You saw Kawata's work."

Could painting a canvas a solid color and adding some squares even count as art? Maybe Iroha could show him something easy he could take back to his dad.

"As long as you don't expect much from me."

Kenta followed Iroha to the back and up a small staircase and got an even better view of that squeeze-worthy ass.

Iroha opened the door. It was one big room with windows all along one side. A sofa sat in front of a large TV, and a small kitchen had been thrown in to the side. An unkempt bed sat in the corner.

Kenta swallowed. He thought they'd go to Iroha's studio, not his home. Subaru definitely wouldn't approve of waltzing into a client's bedroom. Kenta would have to think of some polite way to excuse himself.

Kenta turned and caught sight of dozens of paintings propped up against the back wall. All of them were in various stages of done. There was no doubt the space was for painting, sleeping nothing more than an afterthought.

"Go ahead and find a blank one, and I'll get the paints

ready." Iroha put on an instrumental version of a Lillith song and gathered some paints together.

Kenta switched through the stacks of canvases, but they all had something on them.

"I don't see a blank one," Kenta said.

"You're holding one." Iroha walked over and grabbed another one. "These didn't work out, so they're painted over in white. They're basically new."

Kenta glanced at the one he was holding, which had a faint picture of a cow with some words he couldn't make out because the canvas had been whitewashed.

"Why did you paint over them?"

"No one wanted them." Iroha sighed, then plastered on a smile. "They were fun to paint, but now it's time to have fun painting something new."

Kenta would've happily turned Iroha's forced smiled into something real. But none of Iroha's art looked intact, washed over with a hazy white cloud or half finished, so Kenta wasn't sure if painting would make Iroha smile. Were all artists so picky about their own work?

"Come on," Iroha said. "I got you all set up."

Kenta waited for Iroha to get a few steps ahead before following to the other side of the room. Two easels were set up with a little table of squeezed-out paints and various brushes in jars.

"Do you need an apron?" Iroha asked. "I swear everything I wear has paint on it somewhere."

"I'll be fine. Maybe that'll give my clothes some character."

Iroha smiled at Kenta's sad attempt at a joke before turning to the painting. His foot tapped to the bass line of the song, and he mouthed the lyrics not there. Kenta didn't think Iroha could look any cuter than with his face squished up as he glared at the canvas he worked on.

Kenta took in a breath. If Iroha was putting kids' paintings up on the wall, then Kenta shouldn't worry about him judging him. He could paint the landscape of his village. He'd seen it enough times to paint it. How hard could it be?

Kenta dipped his brush in blue and brushed it on the top half of the painting. Then he added a large tree trunk to one side.

Iroha had stuck a few shades of blue and yellow closest to Kenta, but if he wanted to do a landscape, he needed green. Kenta bit his lip. Green had to be somewhere among the grays next to Iroha.

Kenta pushed his brush into a gray that looked like the shade of the trees back home, then put it on the canvas. He groaned. It didn't look right.

"Don't worry. Have fun," Iroha said.

Easy for him to say; Iroha could paint. Kenta glanced over to Iroha, who was running the bristles of a fine brush up the canvas to paint a large spider leg.

"Yours looks good," Kenta said. "I don't even know if I'm doing mine right."

Iroha shook his head. "You can't do it wrong."

"Well, it's not turning out the way I want," Kenta said.

Iroha put his brush down and leaned over. "It looks good."

"Did I get the colors wrong?"

"You can color it however you want."

Kenta groaned. "I'm not one of the day care kids. You can say it's crap and that I used the wrong colors."

"You want me to talk like one of my old college professors?" Iroha cleared his throat. "The composition of the piece shows much promise. The cool tones of the sky leave many possibilities you can explore."

Kenta laughed. "I was hoping you'd tell me if I'm using green. I went with whatever gray looked like leaves the most."

"You picked right."

"Good." Kenta straightened up a little. "Now how do I paint leaves?"

"Using a fan brush is an easy technique."

"This one?" Kenta grabbed the brush and wet it. "What do I do next?"

"Well, you got your trunk there. So kind of go horizontally in little dips."

"Dips?"

"Kind of here and there along the horizontal." Iroha pointed.

Kenta narrowed his eyes and wiggled his hand. "Can you show me?"

Iroha stood behind Kenta and put his calloused hand over Kenta's. The scent of candy and champagne covered him and turned his heart into the light thumping of butterfly wings. A light buzz electrified Kenta. He wasn't sure whether it was from all the drinking or because Iroha stood so close his breath tickled Kenta's ear.

"See, kind of like that." Iroha's voice came husky and lulled Kenta like the sweetest flower.

"Wow." In a few seconds, Iroha had given the tree a whole branch. "Show me again."

"Last time, then you gotta try it on your own."

Iroha's paint-stained fingers glided over Kenta's once more. He could lean back and be enveloped in Iroha's arms. The bed was right there, and—

Kenta's phone rang.

Iroha backed away.

"Sorry." Kenta pulled it out of his pocket. His heart dropped. Subaru. He bit his lip and answered. "Hello."

"You were supposed to be here five minutes ago. You have a client waiting."

"Shit."

"Excuse me?"

"I got held up." Kenta hoped Subaru couldn't tell he was lying. It felt like he'd just gotten here. "I'll be there as soon as I can."

Kenta hung up and slid the phone in his pocket.

"I'm sorry." Concern was written all over Iroha's face. "I didn't mean to keep you so long."

"No. It's my fault I lost track of time. I gotta run."

"Yeah, I get it."

Kenta wanted to hug him, to feel what it would be like for Iroha's paint-covered hands to wrap around him. Would he accidentally leave a splatter of paint on his coat and all through work, Kenta would see it and be reminded of him? Kenta was already so late and rushing their first hug would only leave them both disappointed. He wanted to leave Iroha begging for more just as much as he was ready to give more.

"When are you coming back?" Kenta asked.

Iroha blinked. "Coming back?"

"To Aphrodite's Castle."

"Getting things wrapped up with the show will take a few days."

"Come back to the Castle soon." Kenta grabbed Iroha's hand, gave it a light squeeze, and whispered in his ear, "I'll be waiting there for you."

8

"Then he's all like, 'Let's table this and circle back next week.' Next week? Can you believe it? Then I said..."

Kenta half listened as his client rattled on about office politics.

Ten minutes until Iroha would arrive. Kenta could last for ten minutes. He'd lasted fifteen days without seeing Iroha. Ten minutes would be nothing.

The soft music in the Onyx Lounge slowed time. Kenta couldn't even get lost in the beat like he'd done with his other clients in the Gold Room. So ten minutes could've been ten days, but time did pass. Especially when visions of Iroha stripping off clothes danced in Kenta's head.

"I need to get going," Kenta said. "I'll see you soon?"

The client tapped his empty wine glass. "Things are getting hectic at the office. It might be a while."

"Don't keep me waiting too long." Kenta winked. "I want to hear what you told your boss."

The client's brow rose.

Kenta's stomach flopped and with so much alcohol inside that it had flooded his thoughts. He must've missed the story when he hadn't been listening. Damn it. It would make the third time he'd screwed up with a client today. He knew better than to get distracted, but anytime the conversation lulled, he'd think of Iroha's breath tickling his neck as he whispered all manner of naughty things they'd do together.

Kenta's client said goodbye, and after a stop to the restroom, Kenta plopped on the sofa in the back. He clutched the plush cushion. If he couldn't stay focused on work with his other clients, how would he be able to keep himself focused with Iroha right there?

Kenta couldn't get distracted by Iroha's collarbones, how his glasses perfectly framed his bright eyes, and especially not how the lollipops he sucked made Kenta think of his dick between those stained lips. Kenta had to pull himself together and sell drinks or else not even Iroha's smile could help him forget about the trouble his parents had gotten themselves into.

Black wing tip shoes approached. Kenta didn't need to look up to know they belonged to Subaru. Kenta stood and tried not to meet Subaru's gaze.

"Iroha's here? What room?" Kenta asked.

"I want you to come with me first." Subaru's firm tone sent Kenta gulping.

Talking with Subaru never ended well. He'd already given Kenta a strike against him for being late the other day. With only two left before he got fired, he couldn't afford it if a client had complained about the lack of his attentiveness. Kenta gnawed on his lower lip. Everyone had off days. Today was his.

He followed Subaru to the little hallway in front of his office.

"I wanted to give you a pep talk before you head out there." Subaru smiled, but it didn't calm Kenta's nerves.

"I'll be fine," Kenta said. "Last week I was back to my usual spot. You don't have to worry about me."

"Do you want me to pull up your day's sales average? If Iroha buys the same amount as his last two visits, you're not getting a bonus tomorrow."

Subaru had never hinted about anyone's rank before. It was supposed to be kept a secret. Kenta's throat burned with his defeat.

Subaru's stern features softened, but he was a big guy and probably looked scary even when he slept.

"Your family relies on you for support, right?" Subaru asked even though he knew the answer. "You need to stay focused."

Kenta nodded. "I understand."

"Good. Iroha's waiting for you in the Gold Room."

"For an hour?"

"Yup, then you got Nakajima."

"I'll make it, you'll see," Kenta said, more for himself than Subaru.

Kenta strolled into the Gold Room, trying to brush off the downward maelstrom of his emotions. The music thumped in time with Kenta's heart. Too bad it couldn't lift his spirit.

He scanned the room and caught sight of Iroha at the

bar. Their eyes met, and the glow of the soft lights made Iroha's sparkle.

Kenta let out a single long breath. He'd thought about Iroha all night—fuck, the past fifteen days. Every time Kenta closed his eyes, Iroha was there. Kenta couldn't throw his obligation to his family in the trash because he couldn't keep clients separate from men he wanted to kiss.

Kenta made his way over to Iroha and slid onto the barstool next to him.

"Teru's concocted the most delicious drink for this week's special," Kenta said.

Teru hadn't, but Iroha didn't need to know. All Kenta had to do was ask for the week's special and Teru would give them both the most expensive cocktail on the menu. Going in strong was what Kenta needed to stay on track.

"I'll have to try it," Iroha said.

Kenta flagged down Teru, and in a few minutes they were served bright-blue drinks.

"This is good." Iroha took another sip. "I wanted to come last week, but you were already booked."

Kenta smiled. "You gotta be faster if you want to get with me."

"I would like that very much." Iroha's eyes grew wide for a second like the words had slipped out of his mouth without him realizing.

Kenta could think of a lot more things he wanted slipping between Iroha's lips. He gulped down a few more sips of his drink as if hoping Kenta would forget what he'd said. He wouldn't.

Kenta put his arm on the bar top and propped up his

head to position himself fully in Iroha's view. Becoming the center of a client's world was key to getting them to spend. Kenta stretched out his other hand and circled the bottom of Iroha's cocktail glass.

"Sold any famous finger paintings from those young Kyoto artists?" Kenta asked, voice low to make Iroha lean in closer to hear.

"I'm sure a few of their parents might think their kid's the next Hokusai. They should get a few more years before their creativity is crushed by thinking about money. You heading back to Oiso tomorrow?"

"I go back every week. It's nothing special."

"Something so out in the county must be peaceful."

"*Peaceful* is another way to say the most interesting thing is when the local stray cat strolls inside the store like she owns the place."

Iroha laughed. His rich brown eyes sent arrows though Kenta's heart.

"We had a cat growing up called Nya." Iroha leaned in a bit closer. "And one time she got into my sister's studio. All her paintings ended up with paw prints all over them."

"They must've made for an interesting show."

"I'm sure the critics would've eaten it up like they do everything she does." Iroha shook his head. "Let's not talk about her though. What's something you're passionate about?"

Kenta went from tracing Iroha's glass to his calloused fingers. How many hours had he needed to hold a paintbrush to get them? How would they feel stroking against Kenta's most sensitive places?

"I think you can think of a few things that get me all hot and bothered." Kenta purred out the words.

Iroha bit his bottom lip and caught Kenta's fingers between his, snapping Kenta's attention from his luscious daydream.

"I want to get to know you better," Iroha said. "But everyone at the gallery interrupted me when I tried."

Kenta kept on stroking Iroha's finger. He could answer that painting was his passion easily, but did Kenta even have any passions? Playing mah-jongg? No. Helping the older residents back home? No. Everything he could say sounded boring.

Iroha squeezed their joined hands. One of his fingers slid down to Kenta's wrist and stopped just underneath the hem of his blazer. Heat flashed up Kenta's neck and face, the soft brushing of Iroha's finger setting every one of Kenta's nerves on fire, screaming for one thing: Iroha.

How could something so simple steal Kenta's thoughts? Of all the things he'd done with other men, something as simple as stroking his wrist left him speechless and begging for more.

"Come on, you gotta have something," Iroha said.

How could Iroha expect him to answer when his finger kept on sparking the flame of desire within him?

"Hiking?" Kenta shook his head. "It sounds so stupid when I say it out loud. But I love letting all my thoughts go and taking everything in. It could be a walk in the city or in the country."

"Taking quiet walks alone in the country were some of the best parts of those middle-of-nowhere art colonies I stayed at. No one around to talk to. Perfect."

A prick of pain stung Kenta's heart. "You like being alone?"

"People usually have ulterior motives when they talk to me."

Iroha's tongue peeked out and ran along his lower lip to catch the last droplets of the cocktail. He slid his finger out of Kenta's blazer sleeve and popped a yellow sucker in his mouth.

Kenta blinked. His arm had never felt so cold.

Then it all rushed back. He wasn't there to be titillated by a suggestive finger underneath his sleeve. He wasn't there to soak up pleasure but to make Iroha spend money, and he couldn't drink with a sucker in his mouth. Kenta glanced to the bar clock. A half hour had passed.

Shit.

Kenta couldn't mentally kick himself enough. Only one drink during the whole time. He'd been too caught up fantasying about Iroha's finger to order drinks.

Kenta leaned in. "Want to go to the other room? It's a little quieter there, and I kind of got a headache."

Daigo had taught him the trick, and Kenta hadn't used it before, but he didn't have time to flirt his way into the other room.

"This one time, sure," Iroha said.

Kenta left the bar, and Iroha followed him to the Onyx Lounge. High, rounded booths made it easy to forget other people existed. They slid into one of the booths, and Kenta put his arm around Iroha's shoulder.

"They have different options here." Kenta grabbed the wine menu and showed Iroha.

Iroha passed the sucker to the other side of his mouth and shrugged. "Whatever looks good to you."

Kenta ordered an expensive bottle, and it arrived a few minutes later. Iroha had given up his wallet easily; maybe Kenta's charm had worked. Though with the way he hadn't even been able to think with Iroha touching his wrist, the art show had to have done well.

"Hey, you can't drink wine with that still in your mouth." Kenta grabbed the stick of Iroha's lollipop and popped it out of his mouth.

Kenta poured the wine for them both and held up his glass. They clanked their glasses together and drank.

All of Kenta's skill as a host left with a single glance at the intensity of Iroha's eyes. Were his parted lips speaking of his desire or simply from the wine? His parted legs begged for Kenta to slip underneath the booth, or was Iroha just sitting? Was his heart thumping in his ears as much as Kenta's?

Almost all the voices swirling inside Kenta's head said to focus on making Iroha buy more, but one voice spoke louder than any other. Iroha would never know how much Kenta truly wanted him unless he acted.

Kenta leaned forward and kissed Iroha. His lickable, soft lips and the lingering tartness from the wine made Kenta explore more. His tongue darted inside Iroha's mouth, then the other voices inside him screamed. If Subaru saw, there wouldn't be a three-strike rule. Kenta would be fired without a second thought.

Kenta pulled back.

"I'm sorry." Kenta hated the need to pretend he didn't crave more.

Iroha pushed up his glasses. "It's fine. I liked it."

"Good. Would you like to go on a hike tomorrow afternoon?" The words came out before Kenta could think. Out of all the things to invite him to, he should have chosen something exciting, not a hike.

"Sure, I'd love to take part in your passion." Iroha laughed.

"Good because I have some other passions I want you to be a part of."

9

"Mr. Iroha, do you like my painting?" one of the daycare children asked.

Iroha walked over to the girl and pointed to her watercolor piece. "You used such an interesting shade of purple. Do you like what you made?"

"I like the kitty." Her pigtails bounced as she spoke.

"Did you have fun?"

"Yeah, I want to make another one."

"You can get started, but you'll have to finish when you come back next week."

She nodded and went back to painting.

Anytime one of the children drew a landscape, a lightness lifted the weight pressing against Iroha's chest. Kenta would arrive soon, then they'd head off for their hike. They could finally be alone without someone wanting to buy a painting or Subaru's watchful eye.

Subaru had made such a big deal about not touching the host, but Kenta had kissed him and they were going on a date. If it was such a big deal, why would Kenta go out on a limb?

"Did you sell one of your paintings?" Chiyoko asked. "You're extra smiley today."

"Am I?" Iroha said.

"Yeah, what's going on?"

"I'm going on a hike with someone." Iroha tried to sound casual, but talking about meeting anyone was far from his standard conversation.

Chiyoko's eyebrow shot up. "Like on a date? Are you seeing someone?"

"Not really." Iroha rubbed his neck. "We kissed, but—"

"Your first kiss! How adorable."

"It wasn't my first kiss."

"Oh, sorry. You seemed like you hadn't dated before." Her words would've hit Iroha's ego more if it weren't for the bitter taste lingering in his mouth.

"I dated in college plenty."

Iroha crossed his arms, hands clutching onto himself, the memory of his college boyfriend still too raw. Iroha had met Eiji in his freshman drawing class. They'd sat next to each other, and Eiji had been the first person who hadn't forced conversations with Iroha. It had been Iroha who had spoken first, and from there they'd been inseparable. Eiji's art had hit Iroha's heart like no other's before, or maybe it had been because every time he would get close, Iroha's heart would pound so much he'd feel light-headed. Eiji had made him feel special, and finally Iroha had felt someone cared about him. Not his sister. Not his parents. But *him*.

Iroha had been so smitten with Eiji that he had invited him home for summer vacation. Everything had seemed normal at first, but then Iroha's sister had come in from her studio. Eiji, the man Iroha had been ready to confess his love for and deepen his relationship with, had turned into the biggest fanboy ever. Everything she'd done, Eiji had followed. It had been so bad even she had told Eiji to leave her alone.

For months Eiji had deceived Iroha to get closer to her.

Iroha swallowed, pushing the memory back to its dark corner, but a lingering pain clawed at his throat. So what if he could count the number of people he'd kissed with one finger? It was better to be careful than humiliated.

"Where did you meet him?" Chiyoko asked. "I want to know all the details."

The gallery phone rang, and Iroha thanked it for ending the conversation. He left Chiyoko with the kiddos and picked up the office phone.

"ABC Gallery," Iroha said.

"I'm from *Kyoto Morning News*. May I speak to Mr. Osumi?"

Iroha crossed his arms, cradling the phone with his shoulder. "What's this about?"

"We're doing a feature on a Kyoto artist and hope you'll be in it."

Iroha glanced back to the studio with Chiyoko and her questions. "What are you interested in?" he asked.

Iroha wasn't sure about answering the questions at first, but the sincerity of the reporter's voice put Iroha at ease and made the conversation flow. Iroha talked about how he'd made his way to Kyoto five years ago. Then they discussed his art philosophy of social commentary disguised underneath fun, Pop art that made people smile.

"Such an interesting point of view," the reporter said. "What are some things you're working on now?"

"I've been playing with a few pieces dealing with spiders."

"Those would complement your other animal pieces. One last thing: could tell me your thoughts on your sister's traveling show?"

Iroha hung up, letting the phone drop on the desk.

Stupid reporters and their stupid questions and stupid tricks to get him to say something about his sister. He opened the desk drawer and grabbed the pack of cigarettes, but they were empty.

He slammed the drawer.

He couldn't trust anyone no matter how genuine they seemed.

When he went to the back, the kids were by the sink washing up. Their smiling faces calmed Iroha's frazzled nerves. He helped them scrub their hands and put their pieces onto the drying rack.

The chime for the door rang, and Iroha looked up to the TV monitor to see Kenta strolling inside.

"Is that him?" Chiyoko asked. "He's cute."

"He's early. He was supposed to come after we were done."

"What? You didn't want me to see him?"

"I didn't want to leave you alone dealing with the kids," Iroha said.

Chiyoko waved her hand. "We're almost done. You go see your boyfriend, and I can lock up for you."

"He's not my boyfriend."

Iroha entered the gallery and smiled at Kenta. Gone were his expensive jackets and tailored pants. Instead, he wore a slouchy pair of jeans and a loosely fitted shirt that made Iroha want to slide his hand underneath.

Kenta picked up one of the 3D-printed *Brain Freeze* sculptures Iroha had displayed near the entry. They looked like brains made into square popsicles.

"These are cute," Kenta said. "It's a play on the English *brain freeze*, right?"

"That's right. I'm glad you like them."

"Did you make them?"

Kenta pushed up his glasses. "Well, technically I submitted the design to a 3D printer."

"That's so cool."

"It was fun to explore something new." Iroha picked up one of the neon-pink brains and pointed to the number next to his signature. "See, this is number forty out of fifty."

A smile spread across Kenta's face and warmed Iroha's heart. At least Kenta liked his art.

"Ready to get going?" Kenta asked. "The train ride there is almost as beautiful as the hike."

"I can't wait to see it."

Iroha said a quick goodbye to Chiyoko, and then Kenta and Iroha made their way to the train station. It would be a half-hour ride outside the city before they could begin their hike.

Iroha watched out the train window as another rolling hill covered in leafy green trees emerged out of the earth. Iroha's shoulders rolled back, and a smile crossed his face. His stays at art colonies had been filled with nature. He'd sit outside and take in the deep sweet zest of the cedar trees, the chirping of birds underneath the constant sound of crickets. Trapped in a bubble of solitude, inspiration would mingle with a deep invigoration that would keep him creating until the morning birds sang. Too bad a gallery in the middle of nowhere wouldn't sell enough for him to live.

Iroha unwrapped a cherry-flavored lollipop and stuck it in his mouth.

"You know," Kenta said, "I play mah-jongg with a few ladies at a nursing home, and they were very jealous I had to cancel."

"I should count myself lucky you're missing a date with them for a date with me."

"They'll be happy I have something new to talk about. Usually all they get is news about the village or what my parents have been up to."

Iroha chuckled. "Your parents must love still being able to see you every week. Mine always try to guilt me into visiting them for New Year's."

"We get along well, and—" Kenta tugged at the end of his shirt and sighed. "The store isn't exactly doing well. So I give them money."

Iroha bit his lip, not knowing what to say.

"Sorry. I wanted you to know in case you ever got

curious why I don't stay with you in the city when I have off."

"I understand. No worries."

The train dove into a tunnel. Everything dimmed for a few seconds before the afternoon sun washed everything in light, but the cabin wasn't the only thing bathed with brilliance.

Aphrodite's Castle had such strict rules about dating. If Kenta's parents depended on him, why would he take a chance? Unless all of it was fake. What better way to make a client feel special than having some intimating yakuza-like goon like Subaru act like kissing and dating weren't allowed? A client who felt like he had a forbidden bond with a host would spend more money.

And it worked so well! Iroha had been so excited about the hike he'd booked Kenta for two more days later in the week.

Iroha picked at a paint flake on his pants, but it didn't distract him from how his heart thumped in his chest like the sporadic flapping of a dying bird.

He'd been so naive.

Kenta flirted and kissed all his clients. He wasn't there for some deep connection with Iroha, only a deep connection with his wallet. Iroha's inexperience had made him read the kiss as something more.

It had felt so real. He should've known no one wanted *him*.

The train slowed to a stop, and Kenta and Iroha got off the train to an abandoned platform station. The mountains towered over Iroha, while the birds laughed at him.

A bright-red Tengu statue greeted them, but its comical, long nose couldn't bring a smile to Iroha's face.

"The trail's this way." Kenta motioned, and Iroha followed.

Even with Kenta by his side, Iroha was alone. His crushed heart pleaded for him to speak, but the words never made it to his mouth.

The tree roots lined the beaten path, exposed and raw to the elements, their interlacing joints turning into a jumbled mess on the dirt floor.

Kenta grabbed Iroha's hand, stabbing his thoughts along with it. How could Kenta be so cruel?

"Look, it's a Joro spider." Kenta pointed and gave Iroha's hand a tight squeeze. "See the web? They build it in three layers, which is atypical for orb spiders."

"You know a lot about spiders." Pretending hurt, but Kenta's casual laugh hurt worse.

Kenta pulled out his phone and took a picture of the creature. "My babysitter was the local scientist. She'd take me to the mountains, and we'd hunt them together. She always said I had a good eye."

"Hmm."

Kenta tilted his head. "Is everything okay? You've been quiet since we got off the train."

"I feel stupid."

"Oh, sorry. I turn into a huge dork when it comes to spiders and bugs." Kenta gave a faint laugh and tucked his phone into his pocket.

"It's my fault for reading everything between us wrong."

"Wh-What?" Kenta's voice broke. He was such a good

actor.

It hurt to look at Kenta, so Iroha turned and picked a spot among the tangled roots to say his confession. "All of this is part of the host act. You're playing the forbidden romance angle Subaru set up. The kiss and now this date. You do it with all your clients. It was fun, Kenta. I had a good time and everything, but I'm going to head back to the train."

Kenta reached out but missed Iroha's hand and only brushed his fingers. "Iroha, wait."

Iroha froze, the desperate tone in Kenta's voice creeping up his arm.

"It's not an act." Kenta's hands covered Iroha's in warmth.

Iroha swallowed, letting the heat envelop him. Kenta's fingers skimmed across his palm.

"If Subaru ever found out I kissed you, I'd be fired. My parents wouldn't be able to survive." Kenta's whispered voice came out like he'd been haunted by the thought.

Kenta's touch turned scorching. His glassy eyes made Iroha's heart scream.

"It's not an act," Kenta repeated. Iroha clenched onto Kenta's shaky hand. "Every time I close my eyes, I see you there. I want to get to know you more. If you'll let me."

"Kenta…" Iroha couldn't draw in enough air to catch his soaring heart. "I—"

"But I can't see you at the club anymore. I can't afford to lose my job." Kenta swallowed, his Adam's apple bobbing. "I want you to be my boyfriend, not my client."

"I want you to be my boyfriend too," Iroha said.

"Really? Then you need to cancel those appointments you made."

Iroha laughed. "Consider it done."

The sweet smell of grass and wilderness filled Iroha's lungs. He reached out and clutched onto Kenta's hand.

"Is it okay if I..." Kenta trailed off, the sultry look in his eyes telling Iroha exactly what he wanted.

Iroha nodded, and Kenta pinned him against a tree off the beaten path. Kenta's tongue plunged Iroha into a pool of sensations. The cherry flavor from the lollipop only intensified the tang of Kenta's taste. Iroha wanted more and could sense every nerve within Kenta begging for the same.

Kenta dropped to his knees. "I've been thinking about this since the first time I saw you stick that sucker in your mouth."

"What are you doing?"

"Hold this for me." Kenta lifted up Iroha's shirt.

Iroha grabbed his shirt, and Kenta's hands flew to unbuttoning Iroha's pants.

"Wait, what if someone sees?" Iroha said.

"It's a weekday, and we're deep enough no one will see." Kenta looked up, his piercing eyes begging Iroha.

Kenta wrapped his arms around Iroha's waist and pushed his face in his crotch. Iroha gulped. He could barely talk, let alone think. Heat swelled in his face and down his body.

"Please, Iroha." Kenta's pleading tone went straight to Iroha's cock, but when Iroha didn't respond right away, Kenta pressed his lips together and pulled away. "Sorry. I didn't mean to push you."

"No. It's not that." Iroha clutched onto the rough bark of the tree to steady himself. "I haven't done this before."

"Oh, you don't have to do anything." Kenta's voice thickened with lust. "Just enjoy it, but only if you want me to."

Iroha nodded, not trusting his voice to speak.

"I want to hear you say it," Kenta teased.

Iroha's cock grew harder. He swallowed; his toes curled inside his shoes. "Go ahead."

The way Kenta intensely held onto Iroha's gaze almost made him worry Kenta would smirk and ask for him to be more specific. Iroha tightened his fingers on his shirt, lifting it higher to get a better view of Kenta. Kenta made quick work of Iroha's zipper.

Cool air prickled against his exposed length, but Kenta's hand wrapped around the base and his tongue curled around the head. Iroha moaned, his head leaned back against the tree. He wouldn't last long. How could he with Kenta's hot mouth engulfing him?

Each of Kenta's suckles and moans drove Iroha closer to the edge. He couldn't get enough of watching Kenta's full lips around him or thrusting his hips slowly into Kenta's mouth.

"Wait, I'm gonna—" Iroha tried to give Kenta warning to pull away, but he only pulled closer, taking everything Iroha had to offer.

Iroha gasped, clutching onto the tree to hold himself up. His breath staggered, and his mind went completely blank.

Kenta wiped his mouth with the back of his hand. "I'm going to have a lot of fun with you, Iroha."

10

Kenta couldn't have asked for someone more understanding than Iroha. He didn't mind how their dates were squeezed into the awkward afternoon hours before work or how Kenta tasted like coffee from the two cups he'd drink so he wouldn't yawn through them. Three weeks together and four hiking dates later, Kenta couldn't believe how each one turned out better than the last. Well, maybe not *blow-job-in-the-woods* good but good in a different way.

Anytime Iroha grabbed Kenta's hand, a warmth would spread through his body, and anytime he closed his eyes, he'd see himself strolling down a mountain path with Iroha for years to come. Maybe it was silly to think like that after only a few weeks together, but anyone who put up with how often Kenta stopped to take a picture of bugs had to be a keeper.

"Iroha!" Kenta waved, spotting Iroha outside the train station.

Iroha always stood out with his long hair and punk

clothes, and with Kenta dressed for work, they'd no doubt be getting a few odd looks. Kenta doubted he'd even notice.

Iroha swirled his sucker around in his lush lips. The gesture went straight to Kenta's cock. Kenta swore Iroha found even more suggestive things to do with the candy. Kenta licked his lips. Maybe the next date he could convince Iroha he wanted to finish the painting he'd started. Then they could move onto the bed.

"Are you going to tell me where we're going now?" Iroha asked.

Kenta crossed his arms. "If I told you, it would spoil the surprise."

"I liked all your surprises so far, so I'm sure I'll love this one too."

Kenta hoped Iroha's words would stay true. All their dates had been things Kenta liked, and he'd made a special effort to come up with something Iroha might enjoy.

The art museum was hosting an exhibition of an artist whose work took Kenta's breath away. Kenta had even managed to snag tickets for her interview. He couldn't wait to see the look on Iroha's face.

"Come on, it's this way," Kenta said.

They made their way down the busy sidewalk. Urban hiking might've offered less opportunity for bug photos, but Kenta enjoyed it nonetheless.

"How many different art colonies did you go to?" Kenta asked.

Iroha pushed up his glasses. "Why do you ask?"

"You talk about them a lot. You must've really liked your time there. I was curious."

Iroha had been guarded talking about himself, but anytime he talked about his stay at an art colony, his eyes would light up, his hands would start moving, and Kenta would finally feel the warmth of them connecting.

Iroha let out a nervous laugh. "Sorry, I don't mean to blab on about them."

"I like it." Kenta reached out, wanting to take Iroha's hand, but they were in public. Kenta could only hope his words would express the longing pulling at his heart. "I want to know everything about you."

Iroha stopped, his cheeks darkened, and his eyes shined with an unmistakable glimmer. Happiness, relief, whatever they spoke clutched at Kenta's heart, and he knew Iroha wouldn't hurt him.

"I want to know everything about you too," Iroha said, words steady, slow, but Kenta didn't need to hear them to know Iroha felt the same.

They walked in silence. Their steps in sync, one after another. Kenta's heart thumped out a steady rhythm of hope with no doubt that Iroha's was beating the same.

After a while, Iroha cleared his throat. "I would go to a different one anytime we had a break in college. Sometimes I would make up an alias once I was there. Almost like a game to see if people realized it was me. It never lasted more than a week, but after that, I could keep to my room and ignore everyone else."

Kenta raised a brow. "What made you want to make up a name?"

Even after a block, Iroha didn't give a deeper explanation.

A part of Kenta wanted to push it. How could he learn anything about Iroha if he didn't open up?

Kenta bit the inside of his cheek.

Iroha hadn't been in that many relationships, and Kenta had already pushed him in other areas. Besides, talking came naturally to Kenta. Iroha would tell him in his own time.

"Can you guess where we're going yet?" Kenta asked a few blocks from the art museum.

Iroha pushed up his glasses. "Are we going to that restaurant you talked about?"

"Nope, guess again."

"A bug museum?"

"Almost."

"A flea circus."

"A flea circus!" Kenta gave Iroha a playful shove.

Iroha laughed. "You always take pictures of bugs. A flea circus isn't that far off."

"I take so many to upload them to an entomology site. Scientists can't be everywhere at once and use hobbyists' photos to help guide further research."

Iroha held up his hands. "Okay, okay, no flea circus. So then, Mister Scientist, where are you taking me?"

"Turn around and you'll see."

The redbrick art museum stood before them, a large banner showing off the latest exhibition.

"Oh." Iroha let out a sigh so long it fogged up his glasses.

"You don't like it?" Kenta bit his lip. "You've probably been here and seen everything before."

Iroha smiled. "But I haven't been here with you."

"You sure? I'm sure there's a flea circus somewhere we can go to instead."

"It will be fun to see the art with you."

They entered, and for a Wednesday afternoon, it seemed packed, but Kenta had never been to the museum before. Iroha made his way to the ticket counter.

"I actually bought them already," Kenta said.

"Oh, okay." Iroha rubbed the back of his neck and stepped out of the line. "Ahh...thanks. So you want to take the tour or..."

"Let's go see the special exhibition."

"We can stick to the usual museum." Iroha turned to Kenta. "You already bought those tickets too, didn't you?" The odd tone in Iroha's voice made Kenta cringe.

Kenta had thought ordering everything beforehand would save them from any awkwardness of a guy buying a ticket for another. It wouldn't have been a real date if they'd bought them separately, but Kenta might've been wrong. All their dates had been free, and all of sudden he was buying everything. Maybe Iroha didn't like it.

"I screwed up somewhere, didn't I?" Kenta asked. "You've probably already seen all the art here enough times. Have you seen the special exhibition before or studied the artist in college or something? Of course you did. She's supposed to be the most prestigious artist of our time."

Iroha raised an eyebrow. "You really didn't know?"

"I mean, I read the little paragraph on the website.

Her stuff looked neat." Kenta sighed. "Want to just cut out and go to a restaurant for lunch instead?"

"You liked her art?"

Kenta nodded.

"Then we can go see it."

Kenta smiled, but Iroha's unease stayed on him like the paint stains on his jeans.

They entered the exhibition and turned the corner to the first painting, and Kenta froze. The image reached inside him, pulled up his darkest thought, and depicted them with photographic realism. Yet it spoke the truth more than anything in reality.

Kenta stepped closer to the work. A lady outside in a garden, but her head was buried in the earth and her body contorted to water the flowers as if nothing was amiss. Each blade of grass and twisted vein was painted with such detail, Kenta felt like he could've stepped inside.

Iroha crossed his arms. "People get a kick out of her surreal horror."

"Is that what it's called?" Kenta asked.

He could've stayed staring at the brushwork for hours, but Iroha already looked bored, so they wandered to the next piece. A person in a suit, but the body had become a tree, hollow, but clearly the image of a person had once lived inside and had vanished the second before.

Kenta noticed his mouth had hung open, then shut it. He glanced to Iroha, sitting behind him on the little wooden bench.

"You don't like them?" Kenta asked.

"From a technical standpoint, they're impressive."

"You do like them?"

"She always had a way to make an impression on people."

"Good." Kenta smiled. "I got us tickets for one of her lectures. If you didn't like them, then I wouldn't have mentioned it, but since you do, that means we can go."

"When is the lecture?"

"It starts in ten minutes."

Iroha stood. "Why don't you grab the seats, and I'll meet you there? I need to run to the restroom."

Kenta nodded and gave Iroha his ticket. They parted, and Kenta entered the lecture hall. Their seats were toward the back. Kenta hadn't been able to snag anything closer. The whole first row was for the press, and everyone there probably knew more about art than he did. Kenta shook his head and remembered what Iroha had said. As long as he liked it, then that was all that mattered.

A pamphlet rested on Kenta's seat. He read how Ichigo Osumi hadn't made a public appearance in a few years. No wonder the lecture hall was so crowded. There had been some biography recently published about her, and the success of the book had inspired her to put together the show.

Iroha sat down. A floral scarf covered his face. It didn't match his usual punk aesthetic at all.

Kenta raised a brow. "What's with the scarf?"

"I was getting chilly. It was the only thing at the gift shop."

"I would've given you my jacket."

"Then you would've been cold."

The lights dimmed, and the announcer introduced Ichigo. She walked to the stage in a frilly red-and-white dress. She talked through the gardener pieces from concept to creation and even showed a few pictures of the early stages. Her voice had a charming quality like a gentle jingle of bells. Yet the more she talked, the more familiar she appeared. Kenta must've seen her somewhere before.

Iroha sunk into his seat, obviously bored. She was someone so famous, he'd probably had to study her work and techniques in college. Dragging Iroha to the museum had been a dumb idea. Kenta filed it away in the "never do again" date category.

Ichigo finished her lecture and opened up the floor for questions. The museum staff would bring the microphone over, and the person would ask their question. They'd ask everything from where she got her inspiration to how long certain pieces took.

The lady next to Iroha raised her hand, and the microphone was brought over. Iroha sank deeper into his chair.

"It's been a while since you've released anything new. I'm curious what you're working on now?"

"My pieces do take a long time to..." Ichigo tilted her head. "Iroha? Is that you, brother?"

Panic struck Iroha's eyes. He didn't reply—he didn't even look at Kenta before bolting out of the room. Kenta followed, half running to catch up.

"What's wrong?" Kenta asked.

Iroha shook his head. "You can't tell me you didn't know."

"Didn't know what? That she was your sister? How was I supposed to? You never told me about your family."

Iroha ripped the scarf from around his neck and pointed it at Kenta. "Type my name into any search engine and every stupid rumor pops up."

"But I didn't want to learn about you through an internet search."

"You're a host. Aren't you supposed to be good at reading people? How can you be so stupid to think I was comfortable? Or were you like everyone else, too in awe to notice?"

"Iroha, no, that's not it," Kenta said, but once the words escaped, he knew it was a lie.

Iroha threw down the scarf. "Since the day I was born, I've never been able to escape her shadow, and you brought me to her fucking show. I thought you were the only one who didn't like me just because of her."

Iroha walked off, leaving Kenta alone.

The museum door shut gently, and Kenta's shoulders slumped.

Iroha was gone. Whatever had happened between him and Ichigo had to have been major. Even if it was, an aching sadness wrapped around Kenta's body like a lover's embrace.

"Wait! You know Iroha?"

Kenta turned to the woman's winded voice and was surprised to see Ichigo before him. She must've run from the stage to the front. There had to be some age difference between the siblings. Kenta could only guess, but Ichigo looked to be nearing her fifties.

"Do you know him?" she repeated, tone as firm as a schoolteacher's.

Kenta nodded.

She reached into the pocket of her frilly dress and pulled out a piece of paper. She scribbled something on it and pushed it into Kenta's hands.

"Meet me here in an hour," she said, clearly not caring if Kenta had other plans. He didn't, but still.

A flock of reporters poured into the room. She laughed off her excursion and herded the reports back to the lecture hall. Like little ducks, the press followed, saving Kenta from their questions.

Kenta rubbed his face. He'd never suspected the art community would be so cutthroat. Yet it had been there right in front of him the whole time. Iroha always talked about sequestering himself to some far-off art colony rather than spending time with his family. It had to be lonely.

He walked out of the art museum and called Iroha.

He didn't answer.

Kenta became more convinced that it was the artist playing dramatics that the reporters ate.

Are you okay? Kenta texted. *Let's talk about this.*

It took a while for Kenta's phone to chirp with a new text.

We'll talk later, Iroha texted.

Kenta rolled his eyes.

Sorry, Iroha added.

Kenta narrowed his eyes. Sorry? That was all the explanation he got? He groaned and pulled out the pink paper Ichigo had given him. If he wanted answers anytime soon, he'd have to meet with her. At least he had plenty of time before needing to go to work.

The words *Nao's Tea* were scribbled between garlands of strawberries.

A café?

Kenta typed it into his maps app and found the

location. Walking would take about an hour. It would probably do him good.

Was it wrong he hadn't spent an afternoon searching Iroha on the internet? Kenta shook his head. No, that didn't feel right at all. He could search while he walked and probably find all the answers he wanted.

No.

He shouldn't have to have strangers on the internet tell him about his boyfriend. Iroha should've come out and told him everything. Ichigo shouldn't be the one to tell him either.

Kenta groaned.

Nao's Tea was on the edge of the historic district. The yellow-plastered walls and dark lattice exterior stood out against the colorful sign but not as much as the police tape covering the perimeter. A very official-looking notice on the door spelled out clearly that a crime had taken place.

Kenta backed away from the door and waited for Ichigo.

She arrived a few minutes later wearing the same candy-colored dress she'd worn on stage. So it hadn't just been part of the show. She approached and gave Kenta a deep bow.

"I can't express how happy I am that you came," she said.

"I have a few questions of my own I want answered."

She squished her face at the police sign. "It's closed?"

"Seems so."

"Damn. This place had the best tea. I was hoping to

stock up while I was here." She sighed. "We'll have to find some other place."

The other place turned out to be a café around the corner. Ichigo got a slice of cake as colorful as her dress, and she paid for Kenta's coffee.

They found a table. Ichigo poked at her cake.

"So are you just Iroha's friend or…" She let the sentence linger so Kenta could fill in the blank.

"We're dating." Kenta tensed. At least he thought they were still dating.

She smiled. "It's so good to see Iroha finally with someone."

"It's only been two weeks, and I think I messed up taking him to the gallery. Is there something between you two?" Kenta took a gulp of his drink.

"You're not in the art community?"

"No. I'm a host."

"Aah, no wonder you look so put together." She took another bite of cake. "You really don't know anything?"

"Is it too much to expect your boyfriend to tell you about them and not have to search the internet?"

"It's hard when you're used to everyone knowing your business. Sometimes reporters will pull out these photos from when I was a kid and I have no idea where they got them. We kind of assume everyone already knows everything. Do you know where Iroha lives?"

Kenta raised a brow. "Above his gallery."

"Thanks." She took the last bite of her cake and stood like she was ready to go.

"Wait! I want to know what's going on. Why did he run when you called to him?"

"Who knows why my brother does anything? You'll have to ask him."

Kenta stood. "You can't leave without telling me anything."

Ichigo sighed. "It's not something I like to think about either. If you want to know, I'm going to need a rose milk tea to get through everything. You want another coffee?"

Kenta had barely taken a drink as it was. "I'm good."

He wrapped his hands around the cup while Ichigo bought her drink. The only time he'd ever felt more out of place was after his first test in college. Kenta shook his head. There was no way middle-of-nowhere high school would have prepared him for even the less hard to get into colleges. All he was good at was talking, and he couldn't even talk with his boyfriend to know what was going on.

Ichigo returned with two drinks, giving Kenta another coffee even though he hadn't asked for it. Maybe she was more anxious than she was letting on.

"So our parents were performance artists, which is probably why we both ended up with such odd names. Ichigo's more the name of an anime character than a person." She laughed, but the sadness in her voice couldn't hide behind her smile. "Our parents slowed down performing when I was born and encouraged my art. They had connections in the art community, and my stuff was praised from an early age. Seventeen years after I was born, my parents had Iroha. That was around the same time I switched to those massive things I still do.

"It took a year to do that first one, and the rumors started that Iroha was *my* child. It was ridiculous. But my parents said even acknowledging the rumor was in bad taste. So we ignored it, and it only solidified it in people's heads. People screamed in my face, calling me a liar, when I would call him my brother."

Kenta's mouth dropped, his stomach churned, and his heart hurt for Iroha. Kenta might've grown up with everyone knowing him, but they knew him and not some made-up rumor.

"That's horrible," Kenta said.

"I made sure the biography cleared all of that up, but Iroha wouldn't even look at it." Ichigo sighed. "He can be so stubborn. On the surface the art world isn't bad, but underneath everyone is ready to backstab you if they think it would put them ahead. He once brought a past boyfriend from college to visit over a break. I was so happy for him, but then it became clear he was using Iroha to try to get me to mentor him. It was sick. From then on Iroha would go to art colonies instead of home. Is there anything else you wanted to know?"

Kenta could've written volumes with all the questions he had, but getting any more answers from Ichigo wasn't right. It was up to Iroha to answer and take the next step, but Kenta finally understood why Iroha kept on avoiding his questions.

"Thanks for talking to me," Kenta said. "I wish we could talk more, but I need to get going to work."

Iroha dipped his paintbrush into the bright yellow and sighed. The painted Joro spider before him only reminded him of how much he'd overreacted with Kenta.

Iroha rolled his shoulders and sighed. Somehow, he'd thought painting would get his mind off everything, but even playing his favorite songs didn't brighten his mood.

He mushed his paintbrush into the yellow paint and swirled it around like a better mood could be found if he rotated it counterclockwise enough times. Nothing could distract from the burned-in memory of the look of wonder in Kenta's face when he'd looked at Ichigo's paintings.

Iroha's thoughts mangled like tree roots. He couldn't even think of how to begin an apology today for the way he'd acted. He'd call Kenta tomorrow.

Iroha stubbed his brush in the water and left it in the dirty cup. There was no point trying to get any real work done. He pulled out the finger paints for the children's session tomorrow and laid them on the workroom table.

He doubted he could stand to do anything more complicated.

The door chimed, and Iroha slapped on his best smile and made his way to the front gallery.

"Welcome, tell me if you need..." Iroha's rehearsed lines ceased when he spotted Ichigo strolling into his shop like a pink parfait. "Get out."

She crossed her arms. "I haven't seen you in three years and that's what you have to say to me? Can't you give me a chance to explain?"

"Why do you think I moved as far away from you as I could?"

"You could at least speak to Mom and Dad, but you don't even show up for New Year's."

"What would I tell them? How all the galleries this year rejected me and that submitting under a false name proved the only reason they wanted me in the first place was because of my family?"

"What do you want me to do about it? Stop painting?"

Iroha wanted to say yes but restrained himself. The bitterness still lingered in his mouth even if logically he wanted Ichigo to paint and enjoy it as much as anyone.

"I just..." Iroha rubbed his forehead. "I specially asked you not to come to my debut, and you did. You barged in during the middle of the press interview. Then jumped in when one of them suggested a photo of us together. Then you kept on answering their questions. It was supposed to be my show. My first real show."

A heaviness lifted from Iroha's chest. When the features of his debut had been posted, all the photos had been with his sister, and in all the headlines, he hadn't been Iroha but Ichigo's sister.

She wrung her hands. "I've been trying to say I'm sorry about that for the past two years. I was in a funk, and the week before, I overheard someone say how I'd reached my peak a decade ago and I just need to go into teaching. It was wrong, and I'm sorry."

Iroha's ribs squeezed like getting the last bit of paint out of a tube. She'd said it. She'd finally said it. After all these years, he'd finally heard her apologize.

He swallowed. Somehow, he'd imagined her apology different, or at least how it would feel after. His world should've been glowing. His creativity tingling in his body and finally everything right. But he didn't feel that way. He felt the same.

Ichigo's lip trembled. "More importantly, I want my brother back."

Iroha outstretched his arms, and Ichigo hugged him so tightly his insides crushed, or maybe it was a part of himself crushing. The part that had held onto so much anger it had ruined his relationship with Kenta.

Ichigo pulled away and cleared her throat. "I wasn't expecting you here. I thought you'd have someone managing it."

"I like running it myself for now." Iroha shrugged. "I might change my mind later."

"Now, show me around your gallery. This future artist wall looks interesting."

"Oh yeah, the children are free when it comes to art. It's nice to work with a group that isn't critical of their work."

Ichigo nodded. "You always bring the best out of an artist. I missed this. The way you look at art is so different than anyone else I know. The best these things would get is the family fridge, but you displayed them next to everything else. That's a chicken, isn't it?"

Iroha shrugged. "I don't know, but it makes me smile. So it doesn't matter."

"By the way, I spoke with Kenta. He's cute."

Iroha's cheeks grew hot. "Yeah, he's a host, so they have to be all stylish. He's down-to-earth."

"He seems like the exact opposite of anyone in the art world."

"Yeah." Iroha's stomach lurched. "I need to apologize to him."

Ichigo smiled. "Go ahead. I'll watch the place."

Iroha blinked. "You sure?"

"Totally."

Iroha only hoped he'd think of something good on the train.

The repetitive chug of the train didn't pull any inspirational words from the deep, dark recesses of Iroha's mind. Words always eluded him. He spoke with his paintings. Iroha sighed. His inability to articulate his feelings was what had gotten him in trouble with Kenta in the first place.

Iroha didn't have time to paint his apology. He shook his head. He'd think of something. He had to. He'd been a jerk and stormed out of what had been a well-thought-out date.

The train stopped, and he headed toward Aphrodite's Castle. He arrived twenty minutes before it opened. It should be enough time to speak to Kenta and not disrupt his work.

Iroha's hands twitched, and his nerves itched for a cigarette, but it was the lack of them that made him so short-tempered in the first place. He swallowed, but the craving didn't leave.

He dug through his wallet for the elevator card. He

held it against the black disk and pressed the button, hoping it would work. Everything about the Castle had been so exclusive, he wouldn't put it past them to program the elevator to correspond with people's appointments. Doubt clouded his mind but lifted once the elevator jolted alive.

The few-second ride took him to the lush Castle entry. White light flooded the space. The flowers and over-the-top chandelier all lost their luster without the purple and blue lights to set off the mood.

No one waited behind the counter, so Iroha pushed ahead to the Gold Room door.

The door didn't budge.

Neither did the Onyx Lounge's.

Iroha groaned and knocked on the door.

"Kenta!" Iroha called. "Anyone, please open up."

Iroha banged against the door, hating how desperate it sounded.

The door opened wide enough for Iroha to see Teru tending the bar, but instead of Kenta greeting him, Subaru stood before him. His sharp eyes punctured the little nerve Iroha had built up. Subaru looked down at him, the black brim of Subaru's hat casting his face in a menacing shadow.

Iroha gulped. If he'd had any doubt the club was run by the yakuza, it all vanished.

"Is there something I can help you with, Mr. Osumi?" Subaru asked, his tone clearly indicating Iroha needed to leave. Now.

"I need to speak with Kenta. I'll just be a few minutes."

"You're not on today's schedule, and I'm afraid Kenta is booked for the next few days."

"It'll be quick, I promise."

"I can't allow you to enter without an appointment. You should be on your way. There will be consequences should you choose not to." Subaru's tone went from passive-aggressive to downright threatening.

Iroha's stomach flopped. "Please, a few minutes."

"This is your last warning, Mr. Osumi."

"I'll be quick—"

Subaru grabbed Iroha's shoulder like a striking snake, Subaru's grip a warning in itself that he could break Iroha in half.

"I'm sorry, Mr. Osumi, but your presence at Aphrodite's Castle will no longer be tolerated." Subaru pushed Iroha into the elevator. "Your card and membership are deactivated. If you set foot on this property again, I will personally see that you won't be able to do so again."

"But—"

The elevator's doors closed, and it made its way to the ground floor.

Damn.

Iroha got out of the elevator and paced around the little hallway on the ground floor. He pulled out his phone and called Kenta, but he didn't answer. Of course, he wouldn't have his phone on at work.

The beep to leave a voicemail rang.

"Kenta, it's me," Iroha sighed. "I'm sorry. I'll be waiting for you."

Kenta yawned and punched the elevator button. After he'd woken up early for the date with Iroha, the last client couldn't have left soon enough. At least Kenta could make it home before sunrise.

He turned on his phone and tapped to listen to his voicemail.

I'm sorry, Iroha's voice came through the phone's speaker. *I'll be waiting for you.*

Kenta narrowed his eyes. What was Iroha talking about?

The elevator doors opened, and curled up in the corner of the entry, Iroha slept. Kenta stopped and rubbed his eyes, almost not believing what he saw.

"Iroha?" Kenta walked over. "Iroha!"

Iroha jumped.

"What are you doing here?" Kenta asked.

"I was waiting for you."

"You weren't here all night, were you?"

Iroha bit his lip, and it was enough for Kenta to know. He squatted, brushing back the hair out of Iroha's face.

"You could've left and come back, you know?" Kenta laughed. "Why are you here?"

"I wanted to say I'm sorry," Iroha said. "I was a jerk and shouldn't assume you know things about me. I kind of screwed up."

"A little bit."

"And you're not stupid. You're smart," Iroha said. "You're smarter than me about a lot of things, especially when it comes to relationships. I really like you, Kenta."

Kenta's heart thumped in his chest. He reached out and interlaced their fingers. "I really like you too."

"If you want, we can go see Ichigo's paintings again. I can answer all your questions on technique or whatever. I could even ask if she'll go with us. She could dress up like a businesswoman and no one would be able to recognize her."

Kenta laughed. "Does she wear those frilly dresses all the time?"

"Not when she paints."

"I guess it would get messy." Kenta traced around some of the paint stains marring Iroha's pants. "You gotta open up and not think I'm going to secretly search up your life story behind your back."

"Got it."

"Good." Kenta gave Iroha a quick peck on the lips and pulled them both up. "Because I want you to meet my parents."

Iroha's mouth dropped. "Really? They know you're..."

"Yeah, they're fine with it," Kenta said. "You know how

much they mean to me. So if you're serious about us, then you'll come with me. They're excited to meet you."

A little voice inside Kenta worried if it was too soon to ask, especially from someone estranged from his family for so long. Maybe it would be good for him.

Iroha slowly nodded. "I'll do it."

"Perfect."

"It's getting late. Maybe we should—" Kenta cut off the rest of Iroha's words with a kiss.

A little gasp escaped from his mouth before he wrapped his arms around Kenta, drawing him closer. Kenta pulled Iroha against the wall, slipping his tongue inside Iroha's mouth.

Kenta hoped the kiss would soothe away any of Iroha's doubts he had to be having to sleep on the floor all night. Kenta felt a bit light-headed when they parted, but it could've been from the lack of sleep.

"I need to get going or else I'll fall asleep on the floor."

Iroha rubbed his neck. "It was silly, but I didn't want to miss you. I didn't get you in trouble by coming, did I?"

Kenta raised a brow. "Why would I get in trouble? You're the one that came to see me. I didn't know you were here."

"Subaru made it very clear he'd kick my ass if I ever came to the club again."

"So you're on the banned list. No big deal." Kenta smiled and squeezed Iroha's hand. "Come on, you can walk me to the station."

Iroha rubbed his sweaty palms on his pants and stared out the train window at the setting sun.

"Don't worry, they'll like you," Kenta said.

"What if they don't?"

"They only care if you're treating me right. Besides, it's not them but the rest of the town you have to worry about." Kenta laughed.

"The rest of the town?"

"Tomorrow we're on delivery duty. You'll meet everyone. Try not to get too tired answering the same questions over and over again."

"Really? Everyone?"

"Dad says everyone wanted a delivery when they heard you were visiting. They all want to meet you, unless you'd rather watch the store with my parents."

Iroha's insides twisted. "Delivering groceries sounds good."

Two weeks had passed since Kenta had asked Iroha to visit his parents. Each day Iroha's nerves had twisted more and more. Lollipops couldn't dull their ache, and anytime he'd talked with Ichigo about it, she'd said how cute it was he was so worried.

Kenta's parents meant a lot to him, so Iroha wanted to make a good impression, but all he could think about was how they'd think Kenta and him wouldn't make a good fit. They would want their son to date someone down-to-earth like him and not someone who dressed like an indie visual kei rock star, or someone with a steady salaryman job, not an artist.

"We're almost there." Kenta stood and slung his duffle bag over his shoulder.

The train came to a stop. The station was more of a platform with a hut for buying tickets. They got off and stepped onto the cracked platform. An older woman in a faded plaid top gave Kenta a big hug before he could even go through proper introductions.

"Mom, this is Iroha." Kenta smiled.

She put her hands on her hips and examined Iroha for flaws. His cheeks burned, but she smiled and elbowed Kenta.

"You never said how adorable he looked," she said.

"Mom, no one wants their boyfriend's mother calling them adorable."

She clicked her tongue and motioned to Iroha. "You see how moving to the big city has changed him. Talking back to his mother before he even says two words."

Her kindhearted tone washed a wave of relief over Iroha. Mrs. Watanabe seemed nice enough, but Kenta's dad would probably be harder to win over.

"Kenta's told me so much about you," Mrs. Watanabe

said. "I'm glad he's finally met someone. He's been working at that host club so long I thought he'd never meet a nice young gentleman to finally settle down with."

"Mom!" Kenta's cheeks turned a soft pink.

"You told me how much you like him."

Iroha tried to hide his laugh, but it didn't work.

They filed into the car. The whole half-hour drive, Mrs. Watanabe told stories about Kenta growing up, no matter how much he protested. The best one had to be when he'd caught a fish by himself for the first time, then when he'd held it, it had flopped out of his hand, and he had cried and wouldn't fish for the rest of the day.

Through each story, Iroha's muscles loosened.

They arrived at the village. Iroha would've struggled to even call it that. Two dirt roads alongside a mountain with more abandoned stores than open.

They got out of the car. Kenta popped open the trunk, and Iroha reached in to grab his bag.

"Kenta, why are you making Iroha carry his bag? He's our guest. You take it for him."

Kenta hid his eye roll but not very well.

"It's fine," Iroha said. "I don't mind."

"Nonsense. You worked hard at your gallery, and this is your vacation. Kenta, take his bag."

Kenta held out his hand to the approval of his mother, and Iroha handed over the bag. He followed them inside the small home. Family photos lined the walls, and the scent of cooked cabbage lingered like a second guest. Kenta put their bags away while Iroha exchanged introductions.

"You're just in time for dinner," Mr. Watanabe said.

"It smells good," Iroha said.

"It's my special Kanto-daki with cabbage rolls. Might be simple compared to what you're used to in the city, but it's made with the best ingredients in the village."

Iroha chuckled, and the smile he got in return told him that Mr. Watanabe probably said the joke a million times and was happy to have new ears to hear it.

Dinner was good but uneventful. Mrs. Watanabe took over talking duties by telling Iroha about all the villagers. With every passing story, Iroha's shoulders relaxed a little more and the smiles became less forced and more genuine.

Mrs. Watanabe yawned. "I'm so tired. I think we're going to bed."

"Really?" Mr. Watanabe's eyebrows rose. "It's barely even—"

She glared at him, and he faked yawning too.

"That's right," he said. "I'm going to head to bed too. It was a long day."

"We'll clean up," Kenta said.

"You guys have a good night," Mrs. Watanabe said.

Kenta's parents disappeared in the back, and Kenta grabbed his plate.

"Did I miss something?" Iroha asked.

"Huh? Oh, them." Kenta sighed. "They always do that whenever I have any of my boyfriends stay."

"How many have you had over?"

Kenta rubbed his neck. "They were just silly high school things. It was easier to hang out here. My parents are more open than others."

Iroha nodded, and they cleaned up while having a

peaceful conversation. Something about it was so simple, but even something as boring as doing dishes became fun with Kenta.

Iroha placed the final dish in the drying rack. "All done."

"It's still kind of early. Want to go sit outside?"

Iroha shrugged. "Sure."

Kenta opened the door and stepped outside.

"Wow!" Iroha stared up at the sky dotted with stars. "I haven't seen the stars in forever with all the lights from the city."

The fresh night air filled his lungs. Something stirred inside him, igniting a fire in his head and a spark of inspiration in his heart.

"You look happy," Kenta said.

"I don't think I've seen the stars in years."

Kenta sat in one of the lawn chairs and looked up. "They are nice. I've seen them every week, so I haven't missed it."

"It's beautiful. I feel like with that view I could paint nonstop."

Kenta laughed. "I think the nearest art supply store is at least an hour away."

"Maybe next time I'll bring some supplies with me."

"My parents haven't scared you off?"

"They seem nice, especially your mom."

Kenta rubbed his temple. "She usually isn't that bad. She must really like you."

"That's good because I really like you." Iroha pecked Kenta's check.

He reached out, wrapped his arms around Iroha's

waist, and tugged him onto his lap. Iroha's muscles stiffened.

"Am I not comfy?" Kenta asked, his whispered breath tickling Iroha's ear.

He gulped. "It's just new."

"Do you want to get up?"

"No." Iroha knew he should've been enjoying the romantic connotations. The stars! Kenta right there! But Iroha's heart was pounding in his chest like a trapped bat.

"Then go ahead and relax some." Kenta pulled Iroha closer, his back meeting Kenta's chest. "See, isn't that better?"

It was better, but Iroha's heart wouldn't slow. He looked back at the stars and tried to not focus on his ass right on top of Kenta's crotch. With his warm arms wrapping around him, breath on Iroha's neck, he couldn't think. He could only let out a deep-throated moan to let Kenta know he was fine.

"Did you always want to open a gallery?" Kenta asked.

Iroha sighed, pulling Kenta's arms around him more. "I wanted to paint. The gallery was because it lets me paint even if my art isn't selling the best. What about you? Did you try to always be a host?"

"The Castle pays well, and the only thing I'm good at is talking."

"You're good at other things besides talking."

"Like what?" Kenta sat up a little straighter. Probably to hide the fact he was getting hard, but Iroha could still feel it.

"You're good at making people feel at ease," Iroha said.

"So basically, a host."

"Yeah, but you were never super pushy with me to buy drinks."

Kenta laughed. "That's because I was too distracted by your collarbones."

"My collarbones?"

"Yours are very nice."

Iroha laughed. "So you have a collarbone fetish?"

"No, just your collarbones are extra nice."

Iroha leaned back and guided Kenta's hand over his heart. "You've always made my heart beat so hard."

"I hope it's out of excitement." Kenta's fingers played with Iroha's nipple through his shirt.

"Yeah."

"Do you want to head to bed?"

Iroha swallowed, a tingling spreading from where Kenta touched.

Iroha nodded, too worried he'd let out a moan if he opened his mouth. He grabbed Kenta's hand and headed inside.

"You tell me if this is too fast," Kenta said.

It took a few seconds for the words to register over the dizzy flood of every voice inside him screaming that Kenta was the only one.

"This is perfect," Iroha said.

Kenta squeezed Iroha's hand as the bedroom door shut behind them.

Iroha rocked back on the stool behind the grocery store counter while Kenta walked the four aisles of the grocery store to fill delivery orders. Iroha had never had such a quiet morning, and a prick of sadness hit his throat when he remembered it would end in a few days. Then it was back to dealing with Kawata and the people who took art as an investment and nothing more.

An orange cat strolled into the store, jumped on the counter, and meowed at Iroha. He smiled and scratched underneath the cat's chin.

"Are you sure you don't want any help?" Iroha asked.

"I'm good." Kenta grabbed a can off a shelf and put it in a bag. "Besides, I know where everything is."

"With all four aisles, it must take forever to find anything."

Iroha petted the cat once more before returning to his sketch pad. After a few minutes, the cat got bored and rubbed up against Kenta for attention.

The door behind him leading to the house opened, and Mr. Watanabe entered.

"Coffee?" He held out a mug to Iroha.

Iroha grabbed the cup. "Thanks."

He took a sip. Even if he was more of a tea person, he wasn't going to pretend coffee wasn't a welcome addition to the morning.

"You're good." Mr. Watanabe pointed to the sketchbook. "I always wanted to learn."

"I'll show you how to draw the coffee mug."

Iroha flipped to a blank page, happy to find the perfect excuse to not drink from the mug again.

"Oh no. I'm too old to learn a new trick."

"No one is ever too old to learn something they always wanted to." Iroha held out his pencil. "Come on."

A smile crossed Mr. Watanabe's face. Iroha couldn't remember the last time his dad had smiled with the same amount of sincerity. Getting a smile at an easy offer to teach a drawing lesson was something Iroha could get used to.

"Just go slow," Mr. Watanabe said. "This is new for me."

It only took a few minutes for Iroha to go over the instructions, and Mr. Watanabe never demanded Iroha held his hand like his son had. The cup didn't look bad at all.

"If you want to make it even more realistic, keep shading. See how the light hits it here." Iroha pointed to the side of the mug. "Keep this area white and go darker to the sides."

"I think I got it," Mr. Watanabe said.

Iroha stepped back, and Kenta approached, a bag of groceries in hand. No wonder such a wonderful man came from such nice parents. They'd done everything to make Iroha feel welcome.

Kenta leaned over the counter and whistled. "Not bad at all, Dad."

"Only because Iroha's a good teacher."

Iroha gave a nervous laugh. "It was really nothing."

Kenta winked. "I think this means Iroha will have to keep on coming over to give you lessons."

"I wouldn't mind," Iroha said.

Mr. Watanabe put down his pencil, took up his coffee,

and looked toward Kenta. "You got the last of the orders packed?"

"Yup." Kenta turned to Iroha. "You ready to be introduced to everyone in the village?"

"Is it really everyone?"

"We did have more orders than usual."

A bunch of villagers still seemed better than whatever Ichigo was dealing with at the gallery.

"Iroha, you want me reheat your coffee and stick it in a to-go cup?" Mr. Watanabe asked.

"It's better to draw with an example," Iroha said.

Kenta grabbed Iroha's hand and tugged him out of the store.

"You know you can tell Dad you don't drink coffee," Kenta said.

"I'll do it next time."

Kenta stopped and the little rocks of the road skidded beneath his shoes. "You really mean that? You don't mind being trapped in a boring village?"

"Boring? It's relaxing and not filled with art critics."

Kenta pulled Iroha into a quick kiss. "Just keep that in mind when we deliver groceries."

Each basket of the bicycle Kenta walked beside was stuffed with groceries. Each villager greeted them when they approached, and each one had their own story of child Kenta adventures. They were all good-hearted conversations. Then the villager would warn Iroha to treat Kenta right before shuffling them out to the next delivery. Each delivered bag made the village of Oiso feel a little more like home.

After a few hours, they delivered the last bag of

groceries and walked back into the late afternoon sun with a job finished.

"I don't think I've ever introduced myself as many times in my life," Iroha said.

Kenta laughed. "Sorry, everyone wanted to know everything about you."

"I thought I'd have to worry about impressing your parents, but it was everyone in the village I had to worry about."

"They're all like my grandparents, so they wanted to make sure I was with the right person."

"Lucky I passed everyone's tests."

"I knew you would." Kenta placed a soft kiss on Iroha's forehead.

"Is that all I get?"

Iroha wrapped his arms around Kenta's waist and pulled him close. Here in a village, away from the city, they didn't have to worry about being seen, and Iroha's kiss emphasized the fact. He slipped his tongue into Kenta's mouth, urging him to do the same.

Iroha could've stayed in that moment forever, but Kenta parted first.

"We got one more chore to finish. I have to check Granny Omi's lab."

Kenta held out his hand, and Iroha linked their fingers together. They strolled over a hill and past the old lab sign. A for sale sign stuck on the bottom looked like a well-worn afterthought.

"It's for sale?" Iroha asked.

"She's been trying to sell it for years now. I doubt it

will be bought." Kenta shook his head. "No one wants to set up anything in the middle of nowhere."

The middle of nowhere sounded like a perfect place.

A large building stuck out in a field with at least a dozen cabins dotted around the main building. Familiarity struck Iroha like lightning.

"It's just like an art colony," Iroha said.

"Really?" Kenta asked.

"It's a perfect match to my favorite in Hokkaido."

Kenta's eyes lit up. "You want to see inside?"

"You have the keys?"

"Yeah, Omi likes me to check every week."

Kenta grabbed the keys out of the lock backs and showed Iroha around. Kenta could've taken a job as a real estate agent telling Iroha the details of the old lab, but while Kenta talked about the things the lab studied, Iroha could only see the lab for what it was to him. A sanctuary.

Kenta squatted and put some paper on the shelf. "You still here?" Dad asked from the counter. "I thought you would've left by now."

"I wanted to get this stocking finished."

Dad waved his hand, a pencil clutched in his fingers. "Leave it. No one's going to come with everything going on."

Kenta stood and walked to the counter. Dad was back to sketching the village stray cat. Iroha must've given him pointers on the whiskers because they no longer looked like droopy beanstalks.

"You better get going or else you're going to be late," Dad said.

Kenta left and took the bike to Granny Omi's lab, though he couldn't call it that anymore. Gone was the sign, replaced with *ABC Retreat* in rainbow letters. He rode past it and to the brightly colored painted cabins.

It had taken so long from when Iroha had said he'd wanted to buy the old lab to when it had finally opened.

Yet Kenta couldn't be prouder of Iroha. He'd finally reached out and taken what he wanted.

Kenta walked around the cut grass, a smile on his face bigger than he'd thought possible and his heart glowing like cherry blossoms. He waved to Granny Omi sitting with a group of men drawing a tree. The whole village seemed to be there scattered among the retreat residents.

"Kenta!" Iroha called.

They hugged, touching foreheads and kissing briefly before pulling away.

"This is so amazing," Kenta said. "I can't believe you're already fully booked."

"Ichigo said she reserved a cabin in an interview, and then the website broke because so many people signed up. I guess sometimes it's helpful to have such an influential sister." Iroha grabbed Kenta's hand. "Come on, I want to show you something."

Iroha took him to the cafeteria. A large Joro spider painting hung along the wall.

"I figured it would be nice to honor the building's roots," Iroha said.

"It's awesome."

Iroha bit his lip. "But that's not what I wanted to show you."

"Oh, where is it?"

"Up this way."

Iroha took Kenta up the stairs and into another room. He opened the door, and Kenta walked inside. The walls were painted in a splendor of colors and designs. Best of all, Kenta could see all of them.

He plopped down on the bed and took in the vibrant

colors. Warmth filled his chest, and he grew weightless, like he floated in the swirls of brush strokes. Iroha lay beside him, their hands interlaced.

"This must've taken hours," Kenta said. "Look at the flowers. They all have faces!"

"This can be our bedroom, if you want it to be." Iroha squeezed Kenta's hand. "Then you won't have to stay with your parents on your days off from the club."

A dizzying, surreal joy washed over Kenta. During the past few months, he'd been giddy knowing he'd see Iroha during his days off, but the idea of being able to wake up and lick his collarbones first thing in the morning sent Kenta soaring.

"Of course I'll stay." Kenta swallowed. "There's something else I wanted to say for a while now. I love you, Iroha. I want to be with you always."

Iroha turned to face Kenta, so close Kenta could see only him.

"I love you, Kenta."

They kissed, and Kenta knew it would lead to a lifetime of more.

Less than one percent of people that read a book leave a review. Be part of Amy's one percent and help others discover *Finding Our Love*. Leave a written review and tell others what you thought!

Dear Reader,

I got the inspiration for *Finding Our Love* when I went to the local modern art museum to see the Takashi Murakmi's traveling art exhibition. Most were these vibrant anime-style flowers that took up whole walls. It was amazing! Since I was already there, I explored the permanent collection, which left me a bit perplexed. Was the different colored raised tile in front of my art or was it part of the floor. The same with parts of the wall. Is this big brown square a feature wall or art. Clearly, some modern art is lost on me, which got me thinking. What is art? Who decides if something is good or not? How is art even priced? So these questions inspired a lot *of Finding Our Love.*

People on my newsletter received most of this story for free and before anyone else. So if you'd like to read my next book before anyone else, subscribe to my newsletter at www.amytasukada.com/free-stuff.

Thanks again!

Amy Tasukada
July 2020

ABOUT THE AUTHOR

Amy Tasukada lives in North Texas with a calico cat called O'Hara. As an only child her daydreams kept her entertained, and at the age of ten she started to put them to paper. Since then, her love of writing hasn't ceased. When she is not penning her next book, she can be found drinking tea in a frilly dress.

Amy Tasukada loves hearing from her readers. You can contact her through her website and also find out how to be the first to read her next book!

Website
www.amytasukada.com